*First Print Run*

# Mute of

## A Dartmoor Murder Mystery

## by Lou Fletcher

*To Mr Ted Sherrell,
with regards.
Louis Fletcher. Nov '17*

# Foreword.

The author is a retired police officer who was stationed at Tavistock, Devon, during the 1970's. He learned the persisting rumour of a horde of Polish gold having been hidden at RAF Harrowbeer, Yelverton, Devon, during WWII. This story is the result of local legend, actual incident, fact, and the author's imagination: but mostly it is a work of fiction.

All rights reserved. Any resemblance between persons, living or dead, is purely coincidental. No part of this publication may be reproduced, stored in a retrieval system, or transmitted in any form by means of electronic, mechanical, photocopying, or otherwise, without first obtaining written permission of the publisher. The author exerts his intellectual and morals right to this work of fiction.

Cover Illustration by Jamers Fletcher.

Prepared for publishing by Richard Fletcher.

© Copyright Applies. Louis Fletcher 2017.

# List of Characters

Mister Leeden...                     A Dead Man

Det. Insp. Frances Steadwell...      Senior Police Officer

Det. Sergeant Robin Allenby...       Steadwell's Deputy

Abigail Cantrell...                  Private Investigator

Simon Brightwell...                  London Gold Dealer

Günter Weismann...                   Geneva Gold Dealer

Kevin Cory...                        Businessman and fixer

Professor Caroline Cory...           Clinical Psychologist

Marion Miller...                     Residential Home Matron

Bill Merriweather...                 Residential Home Janitor

Colonel Leonid Kowalski...           Polish Military Intelligence

Len Dennis...                        Retired Police Constable

Stan Miller...                Self-employed Builder

Selina Leigh..                A Mute, Institutionalised

Harold Leigh...               Farmer and Black-Marketeer

John Jackson...               Handyman and Thief

# Chapters

| | | |
|---|---|---|
| Chapter 1. | Abigail Cantrell | page 7 |
| Chapter 2. | Mister Leeden | page 12 |
| Chapter 3. | Steadwell and Allenby | page 16 |
| Chapter 4. | Interested Parties | page 21 |
| Chapter 5. | Storm Gold | page 23 |
| Chapter 6. | A Very Barren Corpse | page 30 |
| Chapter 7. | Studious Activity | page 33 |
| Chapter 8. | Len Dennis Reminisces | page 38 |
| Chapter 9. | The Mute | page 47 |
| Chapter 10. | Storm Haven | page 56 |
| Chapter 11. | Abi Makes Her Move | page 61 |
| Chapter 12. | Colonel Kowalski | page 67 |

| | | |
|---|---|---|
| Chapter 13. | Dewer | page 75 |
| Chapter 14. | Leigh Farm | page 81 |
| Chapter 15. | Some Dartmoor Legends | page 90 |
| Chapter 16. | Death, Certified | page 98 |
| Chapter 17. | A Penitence of Confessions | page 104 |
| Chapter 18. | Simon Brightwell Comes To Dinner | 114 |
| Chapter 19. | Dénouement | page 125 |
| Chapter 20. | Nice, Neat, and Cosy | page 132 |
| Chapter 21. | Weismann | page 141 |
| Chapter 22. | Dewerstone | page 145 |
| Chapter 23. | King's Man | page 149 |

# Mute of Malice

*A Mute by Act of God is a person who cannot speak, but a Mute of Malice is a person who refuses to speak.*
*English Law.*

## Chapter 1. Abigail Cantrell

Abigail Cantrell needed two men: one living and the other dead. The live one she would be fussy about as she needed his reputation - for the time being - to help her re-launch herself. The dead one just had to turn up and be a nice little earner. Twenty-four years of age with an hour-glass figure, clear blue eyes and shoulder length black hair, Abi could get any man she wanted but seemed to always end up with the wrong ones. No, the live one had to be the right one this time; she'd had enough of the others.

From her spartanly furnished office in the Devon market town of Tavistock she pressed a pre-dial on one of her three 'pay-as-you-go' phones. It was answered by a young woman somewhere in the South-East of England.

"Hi Suzi, it's Abi."

"Abi, how are you darling?"

"I'm fine Suzi, and you?"

"I'm good, but the cops have been snooping here after you. Told them nothing of course. Got a man yet?"

"No, but I have my eye on a certain Detective Sergeant Robin Allenby, one of Tavistock's finest."

Suzi exploded with laughter, "A cop? Make sure you don't talk in your sleep darling, not with your previous for theft and deception."

Suzi and Abi were long established friends who had absconded from their care-home years earlier and been dodging the law ever since. This had thrown them into a merciless world where they'd committed a litany of mistakes and been used by a succession of males. Then they had woken up and realised their own worth.

Now independent and assertive Abi lived on a quick mind, a silver tongue, and her body as a last resort. But she wanted more than survival and Detective Sergeant Allenby might do nicely.

"How is the rural metropolis of Tavistock treating you?"

Abi had been lying low for five months, having run off with the hearts and money of two other men in December 2005. One was a sop she'd fleeced for fun and the other her ex-employer who'd trusted her to manage his makeover business - she'd made off one Friday with thirty-five thousand in cash.

"Tavistock's OK, but it's not forever dear. As you know, I had a few quid when I arrived - enough to buy my Audi A3 convertible and to take out the lease on a nice little cottage just

outside town, then there was the contract on my office here and all the money for a business start-up. I've had to scatter cash to work up contacts for information, and what with overheads and my lifestyle, well, I'm running a bit bloody low."
"Been up to much else?" asked Suzi.
"I keep Tavistock for a false front and Plymouth, with its population of a quarter million, for crime sprees. I always have a Plan B as you know Suzi. I buy stolen bank cards and get stuff and cash-back by 'tap and go'. Always scattering a false trail - all random stuff - but an experienced investigator can work out that random has its own pattern. I use them for a few days and then sell them to some mug in a pub and get back my outlay. It doesn't pay that well but keeps me in clothes and champagne, so I'm still reliant on my dwindling cash reserves.
"And how's the weather in Glorious Devon?"
"Bloody forlorn and nothing but snow all winter, Suzi dear."
"And your private-eye business?"

Seated at the desk of the West Devon Detective Agency where she was proprietor and sole employee, Abi ran a finger across a stack of files.
"Mostly divorce work and who wants a man who's been through the wringer and had his wallet rinsed out? Anyway Suzi, do you want to hear my news?"
"Shoot, I'm all ears."
"As well as a live man I also need a dead one. At the end of last year I was telephoned, out of the blue, by a stranger from London called Simon Brightwell. He wanted to trace any dead males that came to notice in the area and was willing to retain

my confidential services for five hundred up front - no questions asked. There would be another grand if I reported on the right man and five grand for his name and cause of death. Brightwell described the subject as white, about thirty-five years, six feet plus and of very athletic build. He'd last been seen wearing a grey lounge suit and blue tie, which seemed odd for Dartmoor Suzi, but hey, it's a free country. Well, the five-hundred cash arrived by post the following morning, along with his business card."
"Did you Google Brightwell?"
"Yes, but got little back. No photo or description except to say he's a commodities dealer, but the phone number on the card matches the one on his online profile."
"Still, it sounds like an earner, darling. So, where could this dead geezer be?"
"I suspect he's somewhere on Dartmoor and hidden by snow from all the blizzards. It's been bad enough down here but the snow has paralysed the high moor. Now the thaw has arrived it may turn him up, if you get me."
"Sounds too good to be true. Six thousand -five hundred up for grabs and this Brightwell has never mentioned sex. I wonder what he's like?"
They were still laughing when they rang off.

    Abi stood - the precise click of stiletto sounding on the laminate flooring - and walked to the window to admire her reflection. High cheek-bones and full lips, a flash of gold between dark hair and flawless pale neck, and a slender throat leading to the spotless white blouse with its tiny waistline. Dressed in a blue jacket and skirt she looked every inch the businesswoman. She peered out over the mix of independent shops in a miserably wet Brook Street. A passing car slopped slush, the driver craning his neck for a better view of Abi the Diva as she was known by some local men; not that any knew her that well. As she smoothed her skirt over her thighs she spoke aloud to herself, "Robin Allenby, I need to re-launch myself and you may be the springboard, so I'm going to give you some special attention."

# Chapter 2. Mister Leeden

An hour later she was tapping a pencil on perfectly shaped teeth when her illegal pocket radio - the one tuned to the police band - squawked into life. She listened intently as the local police car was contacted by the control room...

*...Golf Two-Two, go immediately to Leeden Tor between Yelverton and Princetown. A walker has found a man's body buried by snow in a cave. The grid is SX 5627 7169*

"At last" she shouted, pulling on her yellow sailing jacket. Scrabbling open a map her finger stabbed onto Leeden Tor a mile south of Princetown. She snatched green Wellingtons, pocket radio and car keys, and was out and driving in minutes. Twenty minutes later she heard the police driver report...

*...from Golf Two-Two, arrived and on foot.*

Ten minutes passed, in which time Abi was approaching the scene. Then...

> *...from Golf Two-Two. I can confirm that a male body is on Leeden Tor. Request CID assistance.*

And a short while later...

> *...to Golf Two-Two, Detective Inspector Steadwell and Detective Sergeant Allenby are attending. ETA twenty minutes.*

Eyes fixed on the road Abi thought about the respectable Robin Allenby who was in his late twenties, tall, blonde, handsome, and an Oxbridge double-first in Law and Politics; she'd already tried to get his involvement but he wasn't interested or perhaps was playing hard to get. 'He seems out of his depth with women' she said to herself, 'perhaps I'm trying too hard – or too directly - maybe he needs a bit of subtlety.' Then her mind turned to DI Steadwell of whom she knew a little, 'Why do they call her Frank? It's a strange name for a woman. They say she's good at her job so I'd better keep away from her – just schmooze Robin.'

From a distance the ragged tor resembled a broken-apart warship on a white sea - the relic of some Arctic convoy that had struggled to an iceberg and beached itself.

Snow crunched as she slewed the Audi to a halt on the moorland roadside south of the village of Princetown and its famous Dartmoor Prison. She began walking up to Leeden Tor,

glad of her boots and jacket in the wind. Halfway up Abi was approached by a uniformed policeman going down, who questioned her sternly,
"Can I help you?"
"I was passing and saw the activity. Anything I can do, officer?"
"Yes. Keep clear while I get the barrier tape" he growled and walked towards his car.

She saw the hiker who'd made the find and realised her chance of information. Seated all alone on a rock and surrounded with three Labrador dogs, he looked pale and shaken. This was her moment before the police and media circus arrived.
"Are you alright?"
"Gave me a fright that's all - just didn't expect it. Came out for the first walk of spring and one of the dogs started barking at that cave over there" he pointed to a craggy outcrop with a black hole beneath it at ground level. "Half-frozen body in there, on his back like he was asleep 'cept when I got close I seen he was all dead and smelly."
Abi gently placed her hand on his arm, "How awful for you – a man's body you say. Another walker do you think? What's he wearing?"
"Dressed like a tramp, a hobo type, and been there a while I reckon. I had to push snow aside so I must be the first. The cave's quite deep but not very high. I used this emergency torch to get a look. Quite upset me it has." Closing his eyes he washed his face with the palm of one hand.

"How horrid my dear, give me your phone number in case you need counselling."

She wanted it as a contingency, but hadn't the slightest intention of helping him.

He rattled the number mechanically and then looked away. She wouldn't get more but he'd confirmed it was a dead male which was a good start.

The uniform returned with his barrier-tape and established the cordon.

"I told you to keep out of the way - CID are nearly here."

Abi didn't have to wait long before the arrival of Steadwell and Allenby.

# Chapter 3. Steadwell and Allenby

"Up there Robin" said Detective Inspector Frances Steadwell. She pulled her car into a lay-by close to Leeden Tor, stopping beside a yellow and blue police Land Rover and a red Audi convertible. Robin recognised the Audi as Abi Cantrell's but said nothing as Steadwell and he walked towards the distant figures.

Steadwell was thirty-nine years of age and had been a police officer for the last nineteen. She was a first class investigator with a keen mind and a dry sense of humour. Her long brown hair blew freely in the icy wind, and her grey eyes were lively and searching. A farmer's daughter who was very forthright and with a no-nonsense approach: at police training school her favourite expression had been "I'll be frank" - the expression had stuck – and she became Frank Steadwell. Married to a local butcher they had two teenage children, Tom aged sixteen and Alice three years younger. Steadwell kept chickens and a vegetable garden and her hobby was cooking good English food. There were no flaws in Steadwell, no skeletons in her cupboard. Frank had made a first-class job as police officer, and was also a loving wife and hard-working mother; but still a good looking woman who turned mens' heads whenever she entered a room. Frank had taken a maternal interest in Robin Allenby, who gave the impression of being afraid of women despite his good looks. She liked him most for his boyish approach to life and least for his humourless adherence to political correctness.

"Let's have a look" said Frank, their boots crunching on powdered snow as they approached the waiting uniform. Glancing back she saw a police forensic vehicle pulling up, and a hearse. Not far behind was an outside broadcast van with antennae, and another police car. The circus had arrived.

Abi had watched their arrival and walked to head off Robin, ignoring Frank.

"Hello Mizz Cantrell" said Allenby, all politically correct, "what brings you here?"

"Oh, I was passing and saw the activity" she lied, fluttering eyelashes and giving a flawless smile, "any way I can help Robin – do anything for you?"

"Not today Mizz Cantrell."

She tilted her head and let the wind pick up her mane of black hair - some strands blew across her face and she used a finger and thumb to delicately remove one from her mouth. Looking back they saw her breath stream out, like she was making a silent whistle or blowing a kiss. Robin gave a snort but Frank thought her attractive.

"Who is that woman?"

Robin flushed deep red, "Abi the Diva, sorry, Abigail Cantrell a private-eye. She keeps bothering me. Yesterday she pushed her chest at me and asked if I would like to take her out? I acted stupid and said I wash my hair midweek but she keeps making a play. How embarrassing."

'Robin, you poor lamb' thought Frank, as she approached the uniformed policeman.

"The body's beneath that overhang in a small cave Inspector. Could be a walker or a tramp; if he was frozen in by the storms he's been there since the end of last year." They knelt in the snow at the cave entrance. Switching on torches Frank and Robin crawled inside a space about fifteen feet deep by three feet high and twice the width of a man. It was as cold as a deep-freeze inside, mind-numbingly cold, the ground was solid and ice crackled beneath them as they moved. Their breath smoked in small white clouds as they squirmed closer. At first Frank thought the body was a mannequin - the result of a poor joke - but as her eyesight adjusted she could see a male corpse lying flat on its back. Closest to her were the soles of shoes and the head farthest away. The right side of the body was still shrouded in drifted snow but the left was emerging from its icy cocoon. He was dressed in an old jacket and trousers and stretched out full length, lying neatly with heels together and the left arm lying down its side - fingers outstretched with the palm towards the thigh. Extending flat out on her stomach Frank inched closer. Pale torchlight illuminated a woollen hat and a face the colour of dirty chalk that was covered in lace-like frost. His pale blue mouth was set in a determined line and his eyes were tightly closed, the lashes glittering with pinpricks of ice.

"Not dressed for winter or moorwalking" said Frank, her speech muffled in the confined space.

"Ordinary shoes, no weatherproof coat and a thin open-necked shirt; he's not really clothed to be out here at all" agreed Robin.

They lay there a few minutes to gain a lasting impression of this man and this place, something personal and visceral, that the later photographs would never convey.

"He could be an end of autumn walker who was taken ill" added Frank, "but something's wrong. His eyes and mouth are closed and that never happens, not even when people die in their sleep. Go out and ask the undertaker to join me."

Heavy and out of shape the undertaker puffed and wriggled until level with Frank, who asked, "What do you make of him?" The undertaker studied the corpse for a few moments, "I've laid out hundreds and hundreds in my time and this man was stretched out after death. Flat on his back, hands down his legs like a soldier on parade, eyes and mouth closed. He's been arranged and no doubt."

"Just what I was thinking" said Frank, her mind turning over possibilities.

"There's something else" added the undertaker, "he didn't die here – he'd been long dead when brought here – say a week or so by the look of him."

"How can you possibly tell that?"

"It's my profession. You'll see if the pathologist doesn't agree, Inspector."

Frank thought 'If he was brought here after death there must have been two or more to carry and arrange him.'

They backed out to see a media broadcast team running up the slope in the pale afternoon sunshine, one of them holding aloft a microphone resembling a large hairy caterpillar impaled on a stick. Forensic officers were erecting a small tent near the cave entrance and down at the roadside other vehicles were pulling up.

"It's getting too crowded Robin - let forensic have a preliminary look then move him to the mortuary at Derriford Hospital, Plymouth."

Twenty minutes later they pulled the body into daylight and transferred it to the forensic tent. Abi got a brief look at a white male of about thirty or so years, with eyes closed in a snow-scattered, pallid face. He was not dressed in a grey lounge suit but an old tweed jacket and a woollen hat, but could have been over six feet tall. She wondered if he'd be worth a grand – maybe another five - and intended having a good stab at it. The undertaker waved an ID label, "Do we have a name?" "Mister Leeden for now" answered Steadwell, and he was tagged and bagged.

The hiker's dogs formed a triangle and began a mournful, drawn-out howling.

# Chapter 4. Interested Parties

Steadwell and Allenby left the scene in the charge of a Sergeant and Constable and made their way back to their car and then to the mortuary. When the cops had gone Abi Cantrell rang Simon Brightwell from her car.
"I've just seen the police recover a male body from a rocky outcrop on Dartmoor. White male, tall, slender, possibly the right age; I'm on it and will ring tomorrow." She omitted the disparity in clothing; why let details get between her and the reward?
Brightwell said, "Keep me informed - I haven't forgotten our financial agreement."
Then Abi telephoned a man called Kevin Cory and arranged to meet for a drink in Tavistock. Cory was a market trader made good, now a successful property owner and venture capitalist; if information was needed he could get it. He was attempting to throw off the semi-villain image which had haunted his life. Kevin had come late to the idea of respectability and was involving himself in charity raising and local politics, fancying himself as a parish councillor - for starters - with better horizons to come. Married to Caroline, a medical practitioner and clinical psychologist, she practised from the Drake Residential Home at Tavistock which they jointly owned. Abi had decided to steer well clear of Professor Caroline Cory and concentrate on Kevin, just as she would ignore Steadwell and work on Robin: either intelligent woman might see through her.

Ж

Three hours later and dressed in a tight black dress, Cantrell entered a secluded Tavistock club. Kevin was already there and they settled down with drinks, careful to talk about charity issues if the barmaid approached.
"You know what I would like to do for you Miss Cantrell."
"Oh yes Kevin but I would never give it away, much better if you have to work hard for it. Now concentrate on business - some information if you please?" said Cantrell, adjusting the shoulder strap of her bra. He gazed at the green and black lace and then returned to her smiling face.
"The cops have a dead body on the moor, some walker or deadbeat snowed up in a cave since before Christmas - any ideas?"
"Let me ask about and see what you think my results are worth" leered Cory.
The darkness gathered outside as they drank and she displayed enough to keep him simmering. Eventually they separated, agreeing to keep in touch, Kevin giving her a wink and a sly pat on the bottom in case she had missed his point.

Ж

It was nine at night and the disinfectant-reeking mortuary was the scene of intense police activity. The body of Mister Leeden was searched but there was nothing on it except some bottles, a map, and some medicine. Steadwell said "Mister Leeden is starting to drip very productively.  Tomorrow, when he's more manageable."

# Chapter 5. Storm Gold

The following morning Simon Brightwell was at his office in London where he operated as a gold dealer and a go-between in transactions beyond his financial reach. He was in his mid-thirties with comfortable wealth but was greedy for more. He received another telephone call from Abi Cantrell, ending "I have one of my best investigators working on the case" That would be Kevin but it sounded good. Dartmoor was far away and wild, so Brightwell would rely on her. He rang off and dialled a secure number in Geneva, Switzerland, direct to Günter Weismann an international gold dealer – a big fish in the gold business - who was hugely wealthy but, like Brightwell, was always greedy. He was all ears and congratulated Brightwell so far. Weismann took care never to be compromised nor show his complete hand to any business associate; as much as he ever trusted anyone he trusted Simon Brightwell, which was only moderately.

After Brightwell had rung off, Weismann sat quietly in his office and played a favourite scene through his mind, the story on how he had arrived where he was today. He was acting the part of his grandfather who had been a trusted vault manager at the Polish National Bank in Warsaw, and had heard the story enough times to recall it by heart…

*…Hitler invaded Poland on the first day of September 1939. Resistance held back the German advance but by the 25th September*

*they were at the gates of Warsaw. The independent Poland was about to be swept away, but the stalled invasion had given an opportunity for the evacuation of Poland's gold reserves. Within the vaults of the Polish National Bank lay 75 tonnes of gold bullion in 12.5 kilo bars, each marked with its unique serial number and a Polish Eagle. A depleted force of Polish army and police had been left to defend the city while the main body of the Polish Army had moved South-East to keep open the so called 'Romanian Bridgehead' - an escape route to neutral Romania for its gold reserves and an army in exile. Trucks had already lined up at the bank, prompting feverish activity in the vaults. Grandfather Weismann was a middle manager but all the top people had fled and he was senior. He supervised the boxes of gold bound for Romanian. Apart from these boxes Weismann oversaw the preparation of three separate tonnes of gold that were going to a Baltic port and evacuation to England in three different Polish warships, where they would be passed to the safe-keeping of Polish military officers already in exile. Weismann saw the three tonnes, each in a separate truck, pull away. He had done his duty.*

*The ground shuddered from artillery shelling and palls of smoke were visible on the city's outskirts. Weismann was alone in the vaults. There were a few more Romanian-bound trucks and these would be the final ones. The Germans were so close and how would he, a Polish Jew, fare? Did a one-way journey to a resettlement camp beckon? The young Weismann was an unmarried man whose elderly relatives had all died; there was no one to worry about. He arrived at a life-changing decision: he would take what he could from the minor gold reserves and get out on one of the last trucks. Dashing back to the vaults Weismann accessed a lesser strong-room where small gold ingots were stored. He began loading one kilo slabs the size of large chocolate bars into a roomy despatch satchel, stopping when it held about thirty. Then he grabbed handfuls of paper money, currencies from all over Europe, and cushioned the bars with them. The bag's strap cut into his shoulder and deciding enough was enough he tightly buckled the front flap. Weismann waved down the very last truck and, hefting the bag, he scrambled into the cab beside the driver and a soldier. He was leaving Poland and would never return.*

*Millions would perish in The Holocaust but one person the Nazis did not catch was Grandfather Weismann and his satchel of gold. Once in neutral Romania he left the bullion truck and bought a robust but unremarkable car, hiding the gold under the rear seat. He also bought old clothing. His position in the bank had called for him to be fluent in German and French and he made his way through Western Romania to Yugoslavia, and then Italy, pretending to be a displaced Frenchman trying to make his way home from a teaching job in Bucharest. Sleeping in the car, he never touched the gold but paid his way with paper currency. Resorting to lies and bribery he laid low at a small Italian village with a border crossing to Switzerland. Befriending the sole Customs Guard he bribed his way across; that was how he arrived in the armed neutrality of Switzerland. Weismann settled down quietly and unobtrusively to a frugal lifestyle. There were complicated political manoeuvrings that kept Switzerland out of the thrall of either Axis or Allied powers and he understood the gold deals being made that supported the war on both sides. Gold was everything and he slowly involved himself with a gold brokering business, first as a messenger and then a courier, until he was trusted enough to handle small deals. Step-by-step he climbed the ladder as a dealer, making official trades for his employer and unnoticed trades with his own gold. He quietly grew in power until the time was right to open his own brokership...*

...Grandfather Weismann made a good marriage and his family and gold business had gone from strength to strength. Günter had inherited the mantle and was an internationally respected dealer – a very big player in the select world of gold trading. He preferred to do business within the law, but if he had to step outside he was an accomplished crook with serious criminal connections: he was a man who always got his way one way or another; and he always wanted more money. Günter Weismann had a stunning secret passed down by his grandfather and he knew about three Polish warships. *"Burza"* or Storm, *"Błyskawica"*, Lightning, and *"Grom"*, Thunder. Grandfather Weismann's story was genuine because a tonne each from Lightning and Thunder had long been accounted for - but never the tonne of gold carried by *"Burza"*, a horde he called 'Storm Gold'. Günter knew it had been placed under the protection of a Polish military officer in England in 1939, but there were tens of thousands of Poles in Great Britain during World War Two, many of whom had later perished: there the trail dried up. The world of gold dealing was small and Günter knew Storm Gold was still missing, but as a precaution he was paying a generous monthly 'pension' to a clerk in the gold clearing section of the Swiss National Bank – an organisation which could track gold bullion movements anywhere in the world. No, he was certain Storm gold was not accounted for, but equally certain it still existed. He was certain because he had a small sample of gold in his possession and a photograph of the ingot from which it had been hacked.

The previous year Simon Brightwell in London had been anonymously contacted by a man using a telephone box in the city of Plymouth, close to Dartmoor. This caller had a tonne of gold for sale. The Vendor, as he called himself, posted Brightwell a small corner hacksawn from a 12.5 kilo bullion bar; this had been accompanied by a photograph showing the sawn corner, the Polish Eagle, and the unique reference number stamped into its yellow surface. Brightwell had forwarded both sample and photograph to Weismann. The sample tested perfectly and the bar number was unique and correct; this confirmed by his informant at the clearing house. It was Storm Gold and no mistake. The Vendor had told Brightwell that if he was interested in doing business he must place a classified advertisement in the pages of Thursday's Daily Telegraph, making an oblique slant at the Hardy Boys Mystery Stories, Volume Five 'Hunting for Hidden Gold.' The classified must say... ***Yes, I want to sell Volume 5.***

So, Storm Gold had surfaced, albeit beyond reach for the present, and if this Vendor had one 12.5 kilo bar he had the whole tonne - another seventy-nine ingots. The thought made Günter Weismann salivate with desire and he wanted them all, so Brightwell posted the cryptic message about Volume

Number Five in the English national newspaper every Thursday. On the third week the Vendor again contacted Brightwell by public telephone. They made progress towards setting up a face-to-face meeting before Christmas 2004. All had been going well and if Weismann could obtain Storm Gold he already had a buyer. The Turk, as he wished to be called, was a ruthless Istanbul gangster controlling the movement of drugs and people from Afghanistan and Pakistan. Determined to enter politics The Turk wished to possess his own gold reserves – to physically have a tonne of gold sitting in his strong-room. This would establish him as a Godfather figure that could dominate lesser criminals and be admired by the sort of business associates who could help him to a bogus legitimacy. He could launder some of the vast reserves of banknotes and murder and cajole his way to controlling a political party and hence government. There were plenty of corrupt politicians willing to help a merciless man with a tonne of gold. Ultimately, could he seize the Presidency? The advantages outweighed the outlay and he was willing to pay a considerably inflated price in used bank notes. The gold was worth between $30 and $35 million but he had vast amounts of illicit cash - black money that would otherwise have to be laundered - and would pay ten times that. Weismann wanted to buy the gold from the Vendor for $25 million and sell to the Turk for $300 million: Brightwell had been promised $3 million which was small change. Günter Weismann was involving himself with a very dangerous person in dealing with The Turk, a person who would kill him if this was a false deal - but Weismann was not leading The Turk down a blind alley; similarly, if Brightwell double-crossed Weismann he would pay with his life – but who could pass up a $3 million fee for a 'one-off' job? Weismann had hired a professional killer as his Envoy; a mystery man with no name or country whom he sourced through a criminal contact. Reportedly, the killer was an accomplished assassin who worked alone. His fee was very large but Weismann was assured he was a complete professional. The killer's identity and background were unknown but he had a reputation as being both ruthless and merciless operator, which suited Weismann. He had had no desire to meet his Envoy; Brightwell could do the donkey work. After liaising with Brightwell at his London office the Envoy would travel alone to Plymouth, and once there go to an agreed telephone box. The Vendor would ring him at a pre-arranged time and from there they would arranged their own meeting. If the Vendor would not do business Weismann's way the Envoy would revert to being a hit-man and kill him, and anyone with links to him, after the location of the gold had been wrung from him by force.

The Envoy had travelled to London and had met Brightwell in early December of the previous year. Brightwell had last seen the Envoy when he left London to catch the Plymouth train; he had been wearing a grey lounge suit and blue tie. Hours later Brightwell received his final communication from the Envoy who said he'd made telephone contact with the Vendor and was following instructions, alone, on a bus to Yelverton, the south-western gateway to Dartmoor. From there he'd disappeared and had been missing for the last four months. Weismann was certain Storm Gold was at this Yelverton location, and was also certain that his Envoy was the corpse called Mister Leeden.

# Chapter 6. A Very Barren Corpse.

The corpse called Mister Leeden had just been examined by Doctor King the pathologist. He was in his office at Plymouth's Derriford Hospital with Steadwell and Allenby.

"What have we? A white male aged about thirty-five to forty who had been very fit and healthy – perhaps an athlete. He was six feet and one inch tall and dressed in an odd collection of clothes. No defence wounds on the hands and no calluses – decomposition has deprived us of all but one fingertip. He has had a lot of dental work. The stomach contained a partially digested meal but I can't say what it was. His reason for death is unknown as yet but, I emphasise, not by natural causes - toxicology may help with blood tests. What I can say is that he died some time before Christmas; anything else Inspector?
"We may get a single fingerprint" remarked Frank, "what about the dental work?"
"Extensive but not done on these islands Inspector, so you will need to circulate charts overseas with professional dental organisations."
"No chance of DNA identification" said Frank, "because we do not have a control sample to match him to. It's easy when relatives report someone missing; we just go around and pluck some sample hairs from the missing persons hairbrush, and we have our control. Then, when a body turns up we just need to match its DNA with the sample and we have a result. Not so

with an unclaimed body, in fact impossible without that control sample."

"You noticed a growth of stubble on the chin and white dust on his back. Why are they important?" asked Robin.

"After death he was stored unrefrigerated and his decomposition was already underway; he had been dead a week before being placed up on the moor."

Frank recalled the undertaker's opinion. He had been absolutely correct.

Dr. King continued, "His eyes and mouth were closed and he didn't do that himself. I think he was stored after death in a cellar or boiler room - the dust smells of oil - and he was kept near machinery."

"What about the marks on his heels?" asked Frank.

"There are drag marks on his heels but none on the heels of his shoes, so the shoes may have been put on his feet after the drag marks were inflicted. This all means someone took him to the tor and arranged him there."

Frank looked at the shoes in their see-through evidence bags, and said, "Those shoes are ordinary street shoes, and they have wear on the broad part of the sole but not the heels. My kids do that to their shoes when they have been cycling, but he has no bike or any cycling kit. So, what *did* he have? An Ordnance Survey map of the area, a bottle of soy sauce, a medicine bottle containing pale seeds, and a blister-pack of cold remedy capsules. No keys, no bus ticket, no money, no wallet or any personal information – nothing. The clothes are strange; a old woollen hat, a jacket of worn tweed material, and a bright green

shirt with a thin, scuffed collar. The trousers were too short and the leather belt fastened too loosely. How can you walk around Dartmoor with your belt not done up properly? He's been dressed on the cheap by someone else - someone who didn't want to buy new and be remembered - it's all charity shop stuff. Someone thought by leaving him there he would be scavenged by foxes and the clothes scattered far and wide."
"Will foxes do that?" said Robin.
"You'll be surprised what they carry down into their dens. Cattle skulls often disappear to foxes - it gives them a calcium lick in the cold months." said Frank. Robin shuddered.
"That person didn't reckon on the big freeze." said the pathologist.
Frank said, "I think it *them;* not one person on their own would have got him up that tor. What about that bleach-smelling cloth that fell from his right armpit and the faint blue marks in the armpit's skin? It's a tattoo, faded and illegible. The bleach cloth was placed there to obliterate it. That tattoo sounds a bit cloak-and-dagger, eh? So who was he, who killed him and why?"
"Well Mizz, not much to go on, is there?"
"On the contrary Robin; what is absent tells us everything. Less is more with Mister Leeden, and did you ever see such a barren corpse?"

Ж

"Hello Suzi dear, good news."
"Abi, what is it? You sound excited."

"The body has turned up, not dressed as he should be but I'm sure it's him. "Enquiries underway as they say. Wish me luck."
"How about the policeman you fancy?"
"Too early to move, but he's in my sights. Bye dear."

# Chapter 7. Studious Activity

Weismann was worried about the discovery of Mister Leeden's body, concerned that the Vendor would be wary and believe it was Brightwell who had murdered him and hidden him in the cave. Brightwell posted a slightly altered classified...

*I still want to purchase Volume 5. You will be in command and leading the tour, which was not my doing. Please contact. You know my number.*

...the oblique reference in Leading the Tour and command would put the Vendor to rest over Leeden Tor - would lull his fears. It worked and Brightwell was again contacted by the Vendor who still wanted to sell.

Ж

Abi Cantrell was doing what she did best – scheming and being a nuisance. A package arrived containing five hundred in twenties and Brightwell's card, on the back of which was written "You are on the right track and I am giving you this in advance. So, £500 you have already had, and £500 for now. Another £5,500 if you get all the information I need." Popping the money into her bag she text Kevin Cory suggesting a meeting that day - her intention was to milk him of information and then dump him - but beforehand she had something else to

do. Driving to Derriford Hospital, Plymouth, she parked where she had a distant view of the mortuary. After Steadwell and Allenby left she saw the last man out - a post mortician's assistant. He drove his sports car past her – she saw a sucker for being suckered by a beautiful woman - and followed him to a pub. 'Easy', she thought, 'single and not nice looking - I don't suppose he has a girlfriend, at least not as pretty as me.' Parking, she strolled towards the pub door, walking past an old-style orange and white VW camper-van that was pulling in, not noticing it or the couple inside; they were much better at surveillance than she. Inside the pub she sat at a table facing the assistant and blatantly flashed her legs.
"Nice car" she said "expensive on fuel?"
He nodded.
"Do you fancy me filling your tank?"
"I'd rather you emptied it."
Their conversation ended five minutes later with her knowing as much about Mister Leeden as DI Steadwell – all for fifty pounds. She could have got it free for sex but didn't fancy him. Now, Sergeant Robin Allenby was another matter, she thought.

Ж

Frank and Robin were in the sitting room of their hotel. Frank said, "We'll let our enquiries run but Special Intelligence think we will waste our time with his dental records, his one fingerprint, and DNA. They think his links are to Eastern Europe or Russia, and the authorities there will tell us nothing.

We have an unknown corpse which made the undertaker remark he had been laid out after death, he's not carrying keys, a wallet or any form of ID, not a watch, not a bus ticket, not even a sweetie wrapper, and the replacement articles of clothing are all devoid of labels. It's perplexing Robin but there is one thing I am certain of - Mister Leeden was killed and then laid out in that little cave - this is definitely a murder enquiry."

Mister Leeden's clothes had been bagged and sealed and it fell to Robin the following morning to start the drudge of enquiries – charity shops, markets, and Dartmoor Prison from where the dead man could have been had been released - it was close to Leeden Tor and his shoes had very little wear on the soles. Frank would concentrate on the non-physical, on people and groups, on local gossip and stories. But first she called at Forensic Science at Crownhill Police Station, Plymouth, wanting to know more about Mister Leeden's armpit tattoo. There she was shown the digitally enhanced photo Ь7Ж3Ø. Frank thought it a serial number and the military connection was inescapable,

'More like Special Services or an elite group – but which group?' She contacted a Special Intelligence Liaison officer at New Scotland Yard.

Ж

Robin visited all the charity shops in Plymouth, Tavistock, and Yelverton, touting Mister Leeden's clothing. Most volunteers could not help him, one even asking, "Have you mugged a scarecrow?" and another, "You wouldn't be seen dead in some of this stuff."  He had some success with a volunteer in a Plymouth charity shop who remembered the woollen hat, and recalled selling it well before Christmas.

Then he had gone to Dartmoor Prison and seen a doleful Prison Officer – a Welshman with a line in dry sarcasm.  The enquiry was a dead-end, and he realised it once he was shown the store from which discharged prisoners were kitted-out on release.  The clothing was of a much better quality than Mister Leeden's and the officer had grimaced at the exhibits, "Oh aye boy, if we sent them off in that sort of guff the left-wing press would be all over us like a rash, see, and those human rights people too.  You have to consider their feelings see, their dignity and all that, like.  No, not from ye'er boy - we're so good to 'em they can't wait to get back in.  Aye, never mind rehabilitation all they want is rehabitation, see, a nice warm bed and three square meals a day.  Oh aye, none of that is from ye'er, boy."

Ж

On the tattoo angle Frank had spoken to Tavistock officers about local military connections, but these had mostly ceased after the war. They advised speaking to the old wartime Yelverton policeman who was in his nineties but still had a good mind. He was Len Dennis and lived with his daughter in the town.  Frank was going to see him the following morning.  Then Robin looked embarrassed, "I've been chatted-up by that Abi Cantrell who wants to make a friend of me; a very special friend. She asked me if I wanted to get inside her knickers - just like that - right out."

Frank gave a wry smile, thinking, 'Poor lamb, they wouldn't fit you.'

Ж

At the same time Abi was sharing a drink with Kevin Cory in a Tavistock pub. Her intention was to give a little whilst getting a lot: his intention was to get her into bed. Both would dole out their information carefully from now on. After Kevin had gone she left a text for Brightwell to ring her at nine the next morning: she was too clever to leave anything incriminating – what with all the hacking - and would report from her office that Mister Leeden had puzzled the pathologist and was a challenge to the police. Finally, she resolved to get Allenby to bed and coax something from him.

Outside in West Street the orange VW camper that had shadowed Cantrell at Plymouth was parked and apparently unattended. Blinds were drawn in the blacked-out rear and the male and female occupants sat motionless over dimly illuminated dials. Cantrell's message to Brightwell was monitored and saved to hard-drive. They spoke in Polish, calling Abi the target and agreeing to be outside her office for the telephone call the following morning.

# Chapter 8. Len Dennis Reminisces

Retired Police Constable Leonard Dennis lived with his married daughter, his wife having died years previously. Frank called by arrangement and was admitted to the house by the daughter, a lady who'd passed seventy and who had the air of a matron or benign prison guard. Frank was shown into a sunlit conservatory where the retired constable was seated in an easy chair and wearing a knitted cardigan, trousers and red leather slippers. Len looked very sprightly for his ninety-plus years and resembled a cared-for baby; all plump and pink with fine wispy hair. Blue eyes sparkled from his round face and he spoke intelligently and in a homely way.
"Please be seated Madam and how may I be of assistance to you?"
"I am dealing with a dead body found recently on Leeden Tor. There could be a military connection with this man. Also, I would like you to tell me about Yelverton during the Second World War?"
"The disruption was massive and unstoppable and we were all caught up in it. There was a war going on and others were dying so we couldn't complain. Plymouth had taken several massive raids from German bombers and the city centre was razed - completely destroyed - so the rubble was brought out to make the aerodrome. It was called R.A.F. Harrowbeer and was operational by 1941. There were loads of supplies on the airbase during the building works, so plenty of stealing going

on. Everything was rationed - petrol, food, clothing - just everything. People today have no idea of what it is like to go without, but there was real want during the war which gave openings for criminals and those who made money from rationed goods; we had a name for them – black-marketeers."
"So the war never ended crime?"
"Quite the opposite Inspector: well, back to Yelverton. Trying to police fit young pilots who could be dead the next day was no easy matter, I can tell you" said Dennis, his eyes staring into the past, "it was like having a tiger by the tail. There was nothing for them except pubs, which meant drunkenness, and womanising. Most women kept their principles but some seemed not to have any at all, and several were left holding the baby - literally. It brought the best out of some and the worse out of others: but that's human nature. Then hundreds of children were evacuated from all over the country and billeted in civilian's houses – people who were already suffering from food rationing had to manage further with nothing extra. The schools were so crowded the kids took turns to sit down - that's how bad it was."
"Were there any foreign airmen in Yelverton?"
"The Royal Air Force ran the base and the first foreigner pilots were Polish who had escaped their own country and been fighting alongside us. We ended up with Canadians, Americans and New Zealanders, but Poles first."

Frank recalled the European connection with Mister Leeden's tattoo and said, "Tell me about the Poles please Len."

"Independent, fiercely loyal, good pilots they say. They kept themselves to themselves in a big house on the edge of the airfield. It was called", he blinked and stared abstractly and then remembered, "Storm Harbour or Storm Haven – something like that – yes, Storm Haven it was. It's still there I believe. I suppose you're going to ask me about the Polish gold?

"What gold? This is all news to me."

"Oh, some tale about a load of gold they removed from Poland before its collapse – all nonsense of course but it did the rounds in the pubs and shops."

"What sort of gold and how much?"

"Don't know but it's supposed to be a big amount in bullion. There was a man looking after Storm Haven for the Poles. He was John Jackson, a sly and shifty weasel. Always driving around a canvas-topped jeep they let him use – petrol rationing was never a problem for some people even with a war on - and he used to bring back fresh food for the pilots, traded from farmers for petrol, most likely. He was doing good business on the airbase where he'd collected cash to get the luxuries of life. Well the Poles took part in the D-Day Invasion in June 1944 and we never saw them again – they flew out and never came back. John Jackson was left to look after Storm Haven and a few months later he disappeared - him and his jeep and the so-called foraging kitty. Left his wife, Jenny, and she pregnant and all. Back then you could travel a hundred miles and start anew, especially with money in your pocket. Well, Jackson was never heard of again and good riddance I say. "

"Was he the big wheel in the black-market?"

Len Dennis settled back and began his tale. "No, but he was working for him - a nasty, horrible bully called Harold Leigh who lived on the moor up the Walkham Valley. Leigh Farm was isolated apart from the prison railway that used to run past - it never stopped there and was only a reminder of the outside world - all decommissioned now and just a lonely track. The farm was abandoned in 1947 and they say the farmhouse has about fallen down, which wouldn't surprise me. Well, he lived there with his wife and their daughter, Selina. Leigh wore his wife to an early grave during the first years of the war and then it was just him and the girl, who was just a kid when her mother died. She's still alive today and lives in a special home here in Tavistock, but she's a mute and you won't get anything out of her. Harold Leigh was in a different league to John Jackson and he was seen by many, including myself, as the centre of crime in Yelverton.
"What was he like?"
"A great bull of a person who had run cattle and sheep on Dartmoor all his life, so his reserve occupation as a farmer exempted him from military service. He'd always been his own man and he put me in mind of those old paintings of Henry the Eighth; a massive and threatening presence looming out at you. Leigh was six feet six if an inch, broad across the shoulders and thick through the chest, with red hair and pale blue eyes over a mean slash of a mouth. I never once saw him without a fat cigar clamped between his teeth and smoke puffing in everyone's

face. Always wore a dropped-brim hat like an upside-down flower pot, and a red neckerchief at the throat. He had ginger mutton-chop side-whiskers that straggled below his shirt collar. Leigh carried a big billhook and was handy with his fists too, and bludgeoned people into submission. Young boys went to him like he was a totem and he organised them like a Fagan into stealing and burgling.

"Did he give you lots of problems?"

"Many a time did he mock me in front of others and say I was too slow to catch a cold, but he was never a stupid person and far too clever to have stolen property on his farm. John Jackson was his runner. He was in fear of Leigh and copied him right down to the red neckerchief and stinking cigar. Harold Leigh would get anything for anyone - whatever they wanted. If the flyers fancied female company Leigh would find some local girls or get some out from Plymouth. He could get whisky and cigarettes and fat cigars for the pilots or publicans, and he could get petrol and motor oil for farmers and garages. Leigh always had a plentiful supply of eggs, meat, and vegetables – there was a war on you know and these things were like gold dust – and he could get nylon stockings and silks, shampoo and scented soaps for women who could pay with money or sexual favours. Harold Leigh was the central criminal pin around Yelverton and could get anything for anyone if he got something in return, because he only helped them as helped him."

Len Dennis's daughter interrupted with tea and cakes. The look she gave Frank told her not to overstay her welcome. They sipped tea and enjoyed slices of home-made lemon-drizzle

sponge, and then Frank pressed on. She had a hunch about Jackson and Leigh, an instinct, and wanted to follow it before the interview was over.
"What happened to the gold?"
"Who knows, but a tonne of gold is hard to move around and I would have heard something – the locals talked about Storm Gold for years but it's all forgotten now and was only a yarn anyway.
"What about Harold Leigh?"
"Not long after the war he was working on his farm when a wall collapsed on him and he was trapped. It killed him. The girl, Selina, she was thirteen and saw it and walked the railway line two or three miles to my police station. She was a dirty and neglected slip of a girl and all she could say was 'wall' or 'fall', I was never sure. She went into deep shock after those few words. That was 1947 and she's been deprived of speech since."
  He lapsed, reminiscing.
"What did you do about the accident, Len?"
"Took her back to Leigh Farm on the rear of my police motorcycle - the place was ramshackle even back then so I was not surprised a wall had collapsed. He'd been using his billhook to clear a drain-hole at the base of a dry-stone wall and it had fallen on him. Leigh was dead all right but I wonder if it had been quick because he'd been alive after the fall - there was frothy blood around his mouth and the post-mortem confirmed he'd been breathing with a punctured lung; there were claw marks in the ground where he'd scrabbled but his injuries were massive and struggling had made them worse. His legs and

back and left arm were buried in stones, and he had injuries to the back of his head. The right arm was crooked up beside his head and the right side of his face turned out towards his right forearm. He had the billhook in his right hand - the arm was broken - but he still had the strength and pig-headedness to flex his wrist and scrabble in the mud. I remember a hole on the tender inside of this forearm from the cigar he always chewed, so he'd burned himself as well. But he was dead all right by the time we got back."

A clocked ticked as he searched his memory, and then Len continued...
"...The CID searched for stolen goods or black-market contraband but found nothing. There was more than £30,000 in an old pot, which was a fortune back then, but Leigh had been a farmer all his life - buying and selling animals with cash - and there was big money to be made during the war. They never found a store of petrol or any illicit property but they took the money and paid it into the police accounts for safe keeping; all proper and above board.
"What about Selina?"
"The CID had it in their minds that she had played a hand in making the wall fall on her father but she was as silent as the grave – not a peep could be coaxed from her after she had mumbled 'wall' or 'fall' to me. The CID wanted the Coroner to class her as 'Mute of Malice', and treat her as an offender and commit her for murder. It was a capital offence back then but she couldn't be hanged because she was under sixteen; but they

would have locked her up for life. The detectives wanted the Coroner to make an issue of her muteness and comment on it – they wanted to take away her right to silence - but the Coroner said she was not ' Mute of Malice' but 'Mute by Act Of God' due to the shock – not a case of *would* not speak, but *could* not speak. They had a medical name for how she was and that was good enough for the Coroner. The farm was abandoned and she was put away in a series of institutions and has been silent to this day."

"Thank you Len, you have been very helpful."

"We all failed Selina Leigh you know. Her mother had been dead since she was very young and Selina lived out there with *him* and that Jackson creature coming and going - no woman to set an example or look after her. Leigh Farm is on the border between two administrations and she fell through a hole in the safety net. People knew about her but never paid her any mind. There was a war going on you see? She never went to school or was seen by the nurse or a doctor, never even baptised. Selina was failed by the system and if you visit her I hope you will not be too hard. Temper your duty with compassion and be the kind person I believe you to be Inspector?"

Len's daughter returned and the interview was over but he told Frank to come back if she needed more.

⚸

Frank went to the town and sat in a café nursing a cup of coffee as she waited for Robin. She thought Dennis had been very useful and *mostly* honest, but he obviously had a conscience about failing Selina Leigh, 'that dirty and neglected slip of a girl.' Neither had she been put off by his smokescreen about the gold. He said he didn't know what amount there had been and then, a little later, slipped up and mentioned a tonne; he even called it Storm Gold whatever that meant? She believed this gold existed and that it may be at the bottom of Mister Leeden's murder, and she also mused where Selina Leigh figured in this. Where was Selina she wondered? It didn't take Frank long to find her. Just as the old policeman had said she was institutionalised at the Drake Residential Home. Frank spoke with a Matron Miller and arranged a visit that afternoon.

Ж

Len Dennis awoke from his midday nap, thinking. 'Storm Gold still causing trouble after all these years. No good will come from this and I just wish it could all be forgotten. Poor Selina, I hope the police will be easy on her – it's caused her a lifetime of worry.'

# Chapter 9. The Mute

Frank was walking up the front path of the Drake Residential Home when spoken to by the handyman-cum-gardener who was trimming the garden with a grass cutter.
"Matron Miller asked me to look out for a lady visitor. I'm the general factotum and my name is Bill Merriweather. I do the gardens and general DIY and keep an eye on the boiler – it can get cold here during the winter so I make sure it's running properly."
Frank took stock of a fit looking man – lean and wirily built with a suntanned face, a healthy person of about sixty.
"Marion Miller - Matron I mean - is expecting you but don't be surprised if you get nothing out of Selina; she's a mute you know and Caroline may not let you near her."
"Who is Caroline?"
"Sorry, Professor Caroline Cory, the resident psychologist: she's taken a special interest in Selina, treated her as a case study, and if anyone could have got her to talk it would have been Caroline. Poor Selina had too much of a shock I suppose."
"What sort of a shock?"
"When that wall accidentally fell on her dad."
"When were you born Bill?"
"1945, but the whole of Yelverton knew about her dad and the wall."
"Do you know who her dad was mates with?"
"John Jackson, the man who looked after the Polish flyers."

"Know anything about the Poles, Bill?"
"No, can't help you there."
"Can you help me with Storm Gold?"
"That old yarn" he scoffed, "no, can't help there either."
Frank continued to the front door only to hear him call after her, "Don't forget - Bill Merriweather. I've lived in Yelverton all my life so if you need local knowledge, I'm your man."

Waiting inside in a dark blue nurses' uniform was a stern-faced middle-aged woman who was wearing a badge saying Matron Marion Miller.
"I see Bill has intercepted you. He's a busybody who wants to know everything that is going on – too nosey by half - but he keeps the place in good order and the boiler served us well all through the harsh months. He fancies himself as an engineer so it's only a matter of time before he blows something up." She was not smiling.
"Also an expert on Yelverton I believe?"
"Born and bred there and cycles in five miles every day, rain or shine. You see him all over on his red mountain bike with a tool bag strapped to the rear. Enough; you want to see Selina but you will need to get past Caroline first, so I'll show you to her office." Matron Marion Miller gave a sniff on mentioning the Professor's name.

The two women walked an airy corridor to a door marked CORY. Matron knocked, and a voice said 'Come'. They entered an immaculate room - orderly to the point of obsession - containing a large polished desk on which was a computer and a telephone. Frank saw a window that looked onto an immaculate garden, and another window into the corridor she had just walked, this was screened on the inside by a venetian blind. There was no paperwork of any kind, not even a calendar. Sitting in a leather chair was Professor Caroline Cory – middle-aged and definitely middle class - her spotless black hair worn in a faultless bob. She was wearing a short-sleeved dress of blue silk, an expensive but understated gold bangle, and a single strand of pearls outside her upturned collar. What struck Frank most was Professor Cory's face; this was tilted in an angle of superior appraisal with thin but perfectly made up lips, and manicured eyebrows which arched above cold green eyes. She looked condescending and pernickety, with immense self-opinion. Frank thought, 'A snob, and an iceberg that I do not expected to smile any time soon.'

Matron made the introduction. "This lady is Detective Inspector Steadwell who wishes to speak with you. While I am here I just wanted to mention the evening menu." Professor Cory appeared to not listen, gazing at her empty desktop. Matron sighed and left, closing the door with a bump.

Once matron had left the professor looked up and said, "Have a seat Sergeant and how do you imagine I can help *you*?" Her voice was slippery with a slightly rough quality which Frank imagined as 'raw silk.' Cory enunciated unhurriedly and perfectly, "I am a very busy person, immensely so", and she stared abstractly somewhere over Frank's right shoulder.

"Good day Professor. I'll be frank - you will understand that I cannot discuss confidential information with the general public which includes *you*, so forgive me if I am not specific. I am investigating a serious offence and my enquiries have led to Yelverton at some time during the past. That's all I can tell you. What can you tell me about Selina Leigh?" Professor Cory glanced sharply at Frank, and then she re-focussed somewhere behind Frank's left ear and replied in a bored monotone. "Selina is seventy years of age and has spent the last fifty-seven in institutions. She is, in common parlance, a mute; an abnormality due to Chronic Aphonia, a medical condition that has caused her the incapacity to speak and which was induced by the bilateral disruption of the laryngeal nerve which controls nearly all the muscles in the larynx. Her condition was not episodic; it was brought about by a single traumatic event. I refer to the sudden death of her father which caused this permanent and irreversible condition. She communicates by means of children's illustrated story books in which she points to drawings – she silently 'vocalises' her thoughts and she communicates with me via drawings in these books - or in scribbled adaptations to the printed figures in them. Selina has capacity, by which I mean that she can hold ideas in her mind and act on them, but she is completely institutionalised and incapable of independence. She additionally suffers from Cynophobia - a deeply rooted fear of dogs - a specific phobia which is most marked at night and when dogs howl in the distance; this will induce an immediate anxiety response. Her phobia is irrational – we do not understand how she came by it - but you must not mention dogs or even form your hand into a claw. I think that is enough information for you to wrestle with.

Come – she's in her room. Be careful, how you deal with her Steadwell, as I have taken a special interest in her case."

They walked to a bed-sit room furnished with a wall-mounted TV, a radio on a bedside table, and a single bed of grey tubular steel. Beside the window a day-chair was occupied by a slender white haired woman wearing a white long-sleeved smock with a high neck collar, and blue trousers. Selina Leigh's white hair was worn short and of non-descriptive style, she smelled clean but not fragrant, her fingernails were short and unvarnished and she was not adorned with jewellery; everything about her spoke to Frank's mind of utility and someone else's convenience. Clear blue eyes were turned to Frank who was saddened to see that they held no hope – no future; worse they had no past and mirrored an empty and meaningless life. Selina looked younger than her seventy years which Frank attributed to a stressless life, yet an underlying tension was evident in her defensive body language. She was very uneasy and living on her nerves, obsessively fiddling with her cuffs and tugging them down if they rode up the slightest amount. Selina looked from Frank to Caroline Cory like a trapped animal. The professor spoke slowly as though talking to a child, "Selina, this is a police lady who wants a little talk, alright?"
Frank drew up a chair facing Selina who had the large picture window behind her. She positioned it fairly closely – not close enough to frighten Selina but with a gap behind for Caroline Cory to step back into.

"Selina, I want to ask you about when you were little, OK?"

Selina nodded.
"I'm not here to worry or hurt you."
A nod, and a glance at was exchanged with Cory, who had retreated slightly out of Frank's vision – Caroline had taken Frank's bait.
"What was your farm like?"
In a drawing book Selina showed a farm building and a passing steam train.
"Do you remember your mother?"
Selina looked confused, then nodded, but there was no drawing of her.
"After she died you were alone with your father?"
She nodded and glanced over Frank's shoulder. Caroline had retreated all the way out of Frank's view and Selina was staring like a worried child at the professor.
"Did you keep animals on the farm?"
Selina turned a page. She had crossed through all the animals except cows, dogs, and sheep, but any illustrations of dogs had their eyes scratched out.
"Selina, did you have a dog on the farm?"
Behind, Caroline shook her head to indicate no, and looked menacing.
Selina shook her head and looked away.
"What was your father like?"
Selina opened another page showing a print of a farmer – the sort of stereotypical image produced by a town-based artist. He

was wearing a dropped-brim hat, collarless shirt, neckerchief, wellington boots, and trousers tied up with binder cord. Onto the illustration Selina had made her own additions by drawing a beer-belly, a billhook in one of her father's hands – the hooked blade exaggerated to look as long as his forearm - and a smoking cigar clenched in his mouth. Oddly, his eyes had also been scratched out in the same fashion as the dogs.

"What can you tell me about your father?"

Frank could clearly see Caroline Cory reflected in the window, staring threateningly at Selina. Cory pressed a finger to her lips.

"Do you remember a man called John Jackson?"

Selina glanced back at Caroline who silently shook her head again. Selina copied the gesture.

"Thank you Selina for being very helpful."

Selina turned to stare abstractly out of the window but Frank already had what she wanted.

    Outside Frank asked, "In what way do you take a special interest in Selina?"

The professor looked at Frank as though for the first time, paused, and said,

 "I have brought considerable time and expertise to making Selina talk. I am an acknowledged expert - widely published and admired - and wanted her to recite a nursery rhyme to a gathering of my followers, but she resisted even my skill. I'm sorry your journey has been wasted sergeant or chief inspector or whatever you are. I thought you police people had better things to do."

"On the contrary – I have learned a very great deal in a short space of time and look forward to my next meeting with Selina."

She walked away without a goodbye, leaving Caroline frowning.

Frank thought, 'How odd. The professor tells me that Selina Leigh is medically incapable of speech and yet, by her own admission, she has spent a lot of time and effort in trying to get her to talk. Either she can talk or she cannot.'

At reception Frank saw Matron Miller who asked, "Did Caroline let you see Selina alone? Didn't think so, she takes a special interest in her - tried to get her to speak but it was impossible. Wanted her to learn a nursery rhyme on account it would be spoken by rote and not challenge her – again useless. I think it was more about Caroline's reputation than Selina's treatment; she wanted her to recite it at a psychology workshop," and she sniffed again.

"Bill seems close to Caroline."

"Too close if you ask me, but I'm only the Matron around here." She cleared her throat noisily and walked off.

Outside, Bill approached Frank again, "As I said earlier, if you want to know about Yelverton ask me. "

As soon as Frank was out of sight Bill went straight to Professor Cory's office and walked in without knocking.

"Did that policewoman upset Selina?"

The professor shook her head and he changed the subject.

"Caroline, I have cleaned the stretched that you loaned to the rescue group practice session." As Bill was leaving he said over his shoulder, "I'm also cleaning one of Kevin's hunting rifles and I'll leave it in his gun cabinet at home, when I'm next working on your boiler."

He did not mention that he had used the rifle when he went deer hunting in Plymbridge Woods with Stan Miller, a builder who was also matron's husband.
He and Stan had used the stretcher to drag out a deer carcase.

Ж

Merriweather went down to the residential home's boiler-room. It was dry and dusty and there were paint and oil cans. Propped against a wall was a canvass stretcher adapted with wooden drag-strips for moorland rescue. He'd done a good job cleaning the heather from the strips. Lying across a table was a heavy rifle with a telescopic sight, and a box of long pointed bullets. He removed the bolt and began cleaning the interior of the barrel with gun oil and a long cleaning rod, humming as he worked. When Caroline and Matron had left he would have another look at Selina's notes and also the map Caroline kept at the back of her files – the one marked with Leigh Farm, and the other with circles and question marks at the nearby Burrator Reservoir. Bill knew that Matron Miller also looked at Selina's file. The police wanting to see Selina could only mean Yelverton and the gold. He would stop digging at Leigh Farm until they lost interest.

Ж

With Bill and Matron out of the way Caroline Cory went back to Selina's room. "You just won't recite for my colleagues will you. Don't be difficult you old bag, because you are passing your usefulness; and if you help Matron, Bill, or that policewoman, or I shall talk about dogs – the sort with big red eyes – the ones you really hate." Caroline made a claw with her hand and Selina nodded acquiescence.

# Chapter 10. Storm Haven

Stone chips flew and dust drifted in the glow of a strip light, as the power tool hammered into the concrete floor. It was choking and deafening in the cellar of Storm Haven as Stan Miller, local builder, determinedly attacked another test-hole. The house was separated from Yelverton by the grassed over strip of the old Harrowbeer runway, and far enough from other housing for him to worry about the noise he was causing. He had recently bought the house on the death of the owner, whose occupancy had prevented digging by anyone. Stan was mortgaged to the hilt and buying the house made no commercial sense but he hoped to find something to clear his problems: a cache of Polish gold. Meanwhile he'd turned his affection to the roulette tables - but the love lavished on Lady Luck remained unrequited and he'd run up very substantial debts, crossing a line at £50k. Two Plymouth heavies had recently called, telling him people die for less. Concrete granules reminded him of crematoria ashes which made him shudder. The cellar was empty except for old paint cans and builders' rubbish, an oil-fired boiler, and a steel cabinet housing a hunting rifle with telescopic sights. Poached venison brought some money but not nearly enough to satisfy the heavies. Bill Merriweather had gone with Stan on the latest shooting trip and helped drag out a dead deer on Caroline's old rescue stretcher. They had butchered the carcase at Bill's house in Yelverton village. Stan kept Bill away from Storm Haven because the old man was too nosey.

Stan had broken through the floors and walls in many places, turning the cellar into a madman's Gruyere Cheese with holes everywhere. A forest of scaffolding bars was holding everything together: some to the ceiling above and others angled to the cellar walls. Inside this tubular jungle were test-bores, piles of grit, and lumps of smashed concrete. Stan Miller was obsessed and he worked in a maniacal and trancelike fashion, driven by the desire to find a tonne of gold which he was certain lay just beyond his reach under the cellar floor. There was no pattern to his work - he just attacked at random wherever he thought the gold may be lurking - the hammer-drill was deafening in the confined space but he leaned his shoulder into his search, and worked with grim determination. He caught movement in the corner of his eye and switched off. His wife Marion had arrived with sandwiches and coffee; he sat exhausted and dust-covered, silently eating and drinking. Eventually Marion Miller said, "The police interviewed Selina today."
"That means Polish gold. I'll have to speed-up."
"I'll have another look in Selina's notes - see if she has given more pointers to Caroline. Bill Merriweather is hanging around - he's interested too. I don't trust him and Caroline together - they're close, if anyone could get close to *her*."
Marion started to leave.
"And be careful this lot does not fall on your head, Stanislaw."

He resumed power-hammering in a cloud of white dust. Stan Miller made no indication of having heard - he was a man possessed by one thought only, in a way that only gold can do.

Ж

It was late Friday evening and only two days since Mister Leeden's discovery. Rain was washing away the last of the snow as Frank and Robin were having a drink in a Tavistock pub. Frank intended to go home and cook for her family, but had decided to stay one more night. "Toxicology have just told me he was poisoned but they can't identify with what. So Robin, we have an unknown male corpse of Eastern European origin and possibly trained as 'special services'; perhaps even an assassin. We've already been through the lack of ID and everyday items. Any luck with the clothing?"
"Only the hat. Did you have any luck with the residential home?"
"That's a nest of intrigue. There's Bill Merriweather the janitor and expert on Yelverton. He has a special relationship with Professor Caroline Cory, and she's an obsessive cold fish - I'll be frank, if my allotment was as tidy as her desk the chickens would walk out in disgust - she's so controlling she needs help from her own profession. The relationship between Merriweather and Cory has side-lined the matron, a woman called Miller. Then we come to Selina Leigh. Now, either Caroline Cory is dim which I do not believe, or she thinks I'm dim which would be a big mistake. She's playing Selina like a piano – the old woman is frightened to death of her. I think

Selina was bullied in her early life and has been conditioned to it. That she was the victim of mental and physical child abuse is pretty obvious but I will prove all that later."

"Going back to Mister Leeden" said Robin, "I have been contacted by the forensic lab and analysis of the dust on his back contains dust, paint, fuel oil, and cement. They agree with the pathologist that the growth of chin stubble indicates he was kept somewhere warm and unrefrigerated for a period of time after death. Back to a boiler room again."

"So we won't be finding his real clothes - they were burned long ago" said Frank. Robin continued, "DNA and the fingerprint are still being looked at, and the dental records have come back as 'substantial work but not from any recognisable clinical source.' Perhaps done in a closed environment - like a military hospital? There is something odd about Mister Leeden. You remember he was carrying a bottle of soy sauce, a bottle of seeds, and thirty flu capsules in a blister pack? The analysis is intriguing. The soy sauce contained a Ricin toxin which is well known in the world of terrorism. It's a killer – remember the release in Tokyo on the mass transport system? The seeds in the bottle were Laburnum and they can be fatal especially to children or the elderly. With the thirty flu capsules – several had been prised from the blisters, emptied and refilled before re-insertion back into the pack. They contain enough potassium cyanide to kill thirty men."

"Potassium cyanide" spluttered Frank, struggling to keep her voice down in the pub, "it's what some Nazis leaders took rather than faced trial. This puts a different complexion on the matter. Perhaps Mister Leeden was looking for the gold and ran into the wrong person and the tables, or rather the tablets, were turned on him. The things he was carrying seem innocuous and would be a good way to transport poisons. He may have been a poisoner who was killed by his intended victim. Good job neither of us had a cold when we searched him Robin; imagine popping one of those flu capsules for a touch of the minor snuffles."

They were still laughing when she went up for more drinks.

Ж

Rain tapped softly on Selina's window, a light but urgent calling to a frightened old woman. What did the police want? How could she reach out to the police lady when Caroline watched her every move? She trusted Inspector Steadwell, even though she had only met her once. Selina felt alone, always had, and her thoughts wandered to her mother's death….

*…he'd made her look in the coffin. After the funeral the house was dead and cold. The shrill whistle of a passing train pierced the stifling silence, then the mist swallowed it and the people in the carriages could have gone to the Moon – she was alone with him. He was shouting that her mother had been lazy and worthless and the house a pigsty; she must clean up. Punishment would follow if she didn't obey. He held up a claw-like hand, breath stinking of cigar. Just her and 'Stinkface' now - she was six or seven years old….*

...sighing,
Selina got ready for bed.

# Chapter 11. Abi Makes Her Move

It was a dull Saturday evening and soft rain was making Tavistock's dark pavements glisten. Abi was on a loose end with nothing better to do - so she decided to do something about Robin. Her enquiries had already told her he led a quiet life and was not one for staying out late, so she intended to intercept him mid-evening. He avoided low-class pubs, not wishing to bump into any villains he may have locked up. She knew that usually on a Saturday he drank a couple of beers in the respectable West Devon Club at Abbey Bridge, and then enjoyed a curry dinner at one of the town restaurants. She also knew that he dined alone and never used his car if he had been drinking. All she needed was to schmooze him off his guard, and then offer him a lift - how could he resist? Once she had him somewhere private she would make love to him and then put him under her spell.

At eight Abi parked and walked through the dark archway of the ancient Court Gate into Bedford Square, and then did a walk-past of the restaurant, satisfying herself that Robin was occupying a booth in a secluded corner of the place. The restaurant was half full of diners but his golden hair was easy to spot. She entered, softly. The murmur of conversation was punctuated by sounds of cutlery against crockery and low background music. The lights were dim and it was civilised and relaxing: perfect for her to make her move.

Robin was unaware of Abi's presence until she slid beside him in the booth. Her skirt and nylon stockings gave a slight swish on the leather bench seat as she moved close, effectively trapping him in the corner. Effortlessly sloughing her expensive red coat, she trailed it on the seat like an exotic pelt. Abi was wearing a white blouse undone one button lower than modesty allowed, and was showing a sliver of snowy lace. Her lustrous black hair had been arranged in an intricate swirl at the nape of her neck and she wore chunky, silver jewellery. Perfume, whispering class and style, washed over Robin like a soft, rich, zephyr.

He glanced around nervously but realised what had so deftly happened. There was a glass screen between them and the next table on which was etched an Indian river scene with a fisherman and a maiden holding a pitcher; these figures were enraptured with each other. Robin looked from this fictitious loving couple to a very real Abi. She displayed a seductive smile; all red lips and sparkling teeth. People on the other side of the screen were just an insinuation through the milky glass - she had him alone and he realised he had snared himself - a victim of his desire to be solitary.

"Hello Abi, what are you doing here?"

"Looking for you Robin, and now I have found you. Buy me one of those nice cold Kingfisher beers won't you, while I look at the menu?"

The waiter was summoned and before Robin could speak, she ordered two.

"What are you going to eat, dear?"

"My usual Abi, chicken Korma."

"That's nice Robin. A man does not have to eat Vindaloo to prove himself - not a real man - I'll have Korma myself, but we ought to have some Pappadums and an Onion Bhaji starter. Don't worry it's my treat - I'm paying."

Oh Abi, I can't let you - rules and all that."

"Forget the rules for tonight and lets enjoy ourselves."

The waiter returned with two bottles of beer, took their order and left. He returned shortly with their starters. They drank cold frothy beer and cracked Pappadums apart, using the shards to scoop thick Mango Chutney and Raita, and fiery chilli sauce. Abi relished the food, sucking her manicured and painted fingertips and licking a spot of chutney from the base of her thumb. When she glanced up he was staring at her and she pinned him with sapphire eyes. For the present they ate in silence - Abi Fox and Robin Rabbit - she holding a Bhaji between finger and thumb and biting and tearing small chunks. He ate abstractly, mechanically, trying to feign disinterest but in truth he was captivated by her: transfixed. Robin had always known she was beautiful and sophisticated, but this was different. Up close and personal was another level of experience with Abi. She was turning it on and he'd taken the bait but would not let her realise. They finished and the things were cleared away.

"What lovely company you are Robin. We should do this more often."

He mumbled agreement.

"Gosh Robin, I felt sorry for that poor man in the cave - been there since Christmas they say?"
"We don't say Christmas Abi in case it upsets other faiths - we say Winter Festival."
"Well, lucky you had the manpower to get him off the moor."
"Person power, Abi."
"Worked like slaves they did."
"You can't say slave because it means that someone else is the master."
"What conclusions did you come to when you and Frank brainstormed the case?"
"The term brainstorm, Abi, is insulting to people who have suffered strokes."
"For goodness sake Robin drop all this crap and let's talk about us. The fact is that I'm a direct sort of a girl and not at all politically correct. I long to be in your arms Robin and wonder why the heck you are playing so hard to get?"

He could not answer and lapsed into silence. The truth was that he found her very attractive but didn't know what to do next, on account of having never having known a woman. Robin Appleby was out of his depth but frightened to show it. Rescued by the arrival of the main course he looked away. Abi played the doting mum, or rather the adoring mistress, and spooned rice onto his plate. Then she selected the choicest pieces of Chicken Korma, from both her dish and his, and arranged them daintily on the rice. Tearing a piece of Nan Bread from the whole she placed this on a side plate within his reach and finally she topped up his glass. Only when satisfied that he had everything did she begin to eat.

Silently, he worked his way through the meal - then dessert arrived.

"I have always had such admiration for the police Robin. All those horrid things you have to witness - like that dead man. You know it will make you poorly if you lock all that angst inside; much better to find a confidant and unburden yourself somewhere quiet and intimate, if you understand me? I have a lovely cocktail cabinet at home and the most comfy sofa. Shall I settle the bill and drive you to my place - it's not at all far?"

He thought about this for a little while and then gave a boyish grin.

"Do you know Abi, I would very much like that."

"Good. Let me settle the bill and we can be gone."

She went to the counter and joined a small queue, thinking, 'success Abi girl - under starter's orders' and then paid with her credit card - genuinely her own one and with funds to back it. Pocketing two foil-wrapped mints she turned back. He was gone! 'You bloody fool Abigail Cantrell. You were too much the floozy' she chided herself. Storming out she scanned the street and then drove past his place, but it was shrouded in darkness. 'You wait Robin - this is bloody personal now and you will be mine.'

She drove home, not in triumph and anticipation, but defeated for the present.

Ж

"Suzi dear, it's me again."
"What's happened? You sound all stressed out."
"That bloody Sergeant is what *hasn't* happened. I put it on a plate for him in a restaurant - metaphorically not literally you understand - and while I was paying the bill he ran off through a side door."
"Is he gay Abi?"
"Don't think so, not the way he was gazing into my eyes; he had to look away to save himself. No not gay - I think he's a virgin."
"I've heard about those type of men. They get very set in their ways - they say it becomes a sort of religion with them, you know, not to give in."
"Well, he's going to give in to me, one way or another, even if I need to kidnap him. I'm going to seduce him and then I'm going to rule him."
"What a feather in your cap that would be - a cop with a cherry on it - it would be like defrocking a priest, darling."
"Oh Suzi, did I ever tell you about the Rector in Royal Tunbridge Wells..?"

# Chapter 12. Colonel Kowalski

The weekend passed by without any progress by the police, but the couple in their orange camper-van had successfully followed several lines of enquiry. They found Storm Haven and witnessed the comings and goings of the Millers; they had walked to Leeden Tor and photographed the cave; and they had also followed Abigail Cantrell and intercepted her telephone and text messages. They were regular soldiers of the Republic of Poland - they were military intelligence and on active service. The camper van was bristling with electronic equipment. They also carried firearms in it, including a powerful snipers rifle with a telescopic sight.

Ж

Frank enjoyed family life and returned on Monday morning refreshed and ready. She was sitting in a Tavistock in a café at Russell Street going over notes and planning the week ,unaware of a man standing over her table until he sat, uninvited.
"Hello Detective Inspector Frances Steadwell– I am Colonel Leonid Kowalski of Polish Military Intelligence."
She saw a man the same age as her – late thirties –who spoke good English with a slight accent. He exuded confidence, had broad shoulders and a mane of silver hair, and was good looking in a way both rugged and urbane. She thought him accustomed to obedience. Frank eyed him coldly.

"What do you want?"
"I want a person at present unidentified. I think we want the same person for different reasons," he said in a reasonable and slightly superior manner, "you want someone for a murder and I want someone for missing gold. This may be the same person Inspector, or do I call you Frank?"
"I'll be frank alright. You have plonked down at my table and I don't know you from Adam. Why should I believe you?"
"Talk to the Polish Embassy in London, where I am attached. They will confirm."
'A spy from military intelligence' she thought, reminding herself to be very careful in her dealings with this man.
"Colonel Kowalski, if you wish to establish your credentials *you* do the running." Frank thought of her chickens that had been given names by the children.
"Get my Special Branch to pass me the code word 'Florence and Matilda'. Good day." She turned back to her work.
Kowalski gave a thin, lopsided smile, and walked away.

Then she went to the police station to follow progress on DNA and the fingerprint but the enquiry had petered out, as if Mister Leeden had never existed. Also they were coming up against an invisible wall concerning the armpit tattoo **Ь7Ж3Ø**. She spoke with an Eastern European Liaison Officer at New Scotland Yard who told her the characters were definitely from the Cyrillic alphabet, and used, amongst others, by the Russian, Slavic, and Serbo-Croatian cultures.

"As such these characters are a random selection and do not spell anything - but are definitely recognition symbols by persons or organisations unknown. It could be identification for a gang of mercenaries or government-approved murderers. If so, they are dangerous people and they will kill without thinking."

She then contacted Special Branch and received the message, "Colonel Kowalski says 'Florence and Matilda' and he will meet you for lunch in The Bedford Hotel, Tavistock - twelve thirty. Be sharp."
'Cheeky bugger' she thought, reminding herself to be late.

Ж

Meanwhile Abi Cantrell had contrived to bump into Bill Merriweather in the grounds of the Drake Home. She tried the blue eye treatment on him for information, but quickly realised that offering the old man sex would be a waste of time. So, Abi worked on Bill Merriweather's ego. Resting her hand on his arm she paid compliments about his gardening and knowledge of local history and asking why the police were interested in Yelverton. He played the yokel card.
"Blimey Miss, nobody tells me nought and I don't know ought, not Billy Boy."
She gave up, deciding to have another try at Robin Allenby. Bill smiled as she flounced off.

'Bloody newcomer, you'll have to get out of bed a lot earlier to make a fool of me.'

Ж

His gaze lingered too long on her breasts as Kowalski poured iced water for Frank.
They were seated in the restaurant of The Bedford Hotel. 'You are handsome, but terribly sure of yourself' she thought as she ordered lamb. Kowalski reached across the table and took her hand, noticing it's roughness of palm and short fingernails.
"Manual work?" he enquired.
"My husband and I keep chickens and grow vegetables."
"Do call me Leon. You are a very attractive lady and I hope your husband is taking good care of you?" He smiled, shark-like, finger resting on her wedding ring.
She did not intend to shrink from his touch, saying, "I'll be frank. My husband looks after me in a way you won't understand. So, I'll speak in a way you will; remove your hand or I'll snap off your finger and poke it in your eye?"
"I don't understand?"
"Understand this: touch me like that again and I'll break your arm Colonel, diplomatic privilege or not."
He withdrew his roving hand, "Very sorry but I have to try everything."
"Try again at your peril. So leave out the guff - what exactly do you want Kowalski?"

"I want us to work together. You want your murderer and we want our gold, so if we cut a few corners will it matter?"
"The law always matters," snapped Frank, thinking, 'Typical military – so focussed on the end result that they treat people as objects. I'd better get the murderer before you: but the existence of the gold is confirmed.'
Kowalski thought, 'Typical police – they worry so much about rights that it makes them righteous.'
 They ate lamb and made small-talk.

   Kowalski kept secret that in 1941 the gold had been transported to Yelverton in twenty wooden boxes by a Polish air squadron. These were marked *'Aircraft Parts. Property of Free Polish Airforce."* Each box was marked with the Polish eagle and held four 12.5 kilo ingots; so 50 kilos or 110 pounds weight in every box, multiplied by twenty boxes - one tonne of pure gold in eighty ingots. The boxes were strong and roomy storage containers in grey painted wood and it took two or three men to move and handle them. Kowalski had long known about the large villa-type house at Yelverton named Storm Haven where the gold had been buried in the spacious cellar, in a pit measuring four metres, by four metres, by more than one metre deep, that had been covertly excavated by the Polish fighter pilots. Covered with silk parachutes and then a tarpaulin, the flyers had concreted over the boxes for later recovery, after having been sworn to secrecy. The house was managed by John Jackson who had watched and snooped and found the gold's hiding place: he was in charge of the empty house after the squadron left for France in 1944. All the pilots were killed except one, who had been a prisoner-of-war. Polish Military Intelligence only learned of the gold's hiding place in 1945 when the surviving pilot had been freed. By then Jackson was missing and the house bought by a Mrs Paling's family; she had only recently died and it was now owned by Stanislaw Miller. This meant the house had either been emptied of gold by Jackson, or it was still in the cellar. If still alive Jackson would be in his eighties or nineties and Kowalski doubted ever finding him. He suspected the gold would not be found in Storm Haven – its whereabouts would remain a mystery, for now.

Kowalski did not tell Frank he already had two agents in Tavistock driving an orange and white VW camper; neither did he tell he had recruited a local Tavistock person as his spy. Nor did Kowalski reveal about the clerk at the Swiss Gold Clearing Office on the payroll of the Swiss gold dealer, one Günter Weismann. Kowalski had explained to the clerk what could happen to his family and turned him into a double agent. Kowalski knew all there was to know about Weismann, in whom he'd invested a lot of time. Finally, Kowalski also knew about Abigail Cantrell and her phone messages to Simon Brightwell, another gold dealer who was a business associate of Weismann. Kowalski and Frank enjoyed their small-talk and roast lamb and then went separate ways each carrying separate thoughts, realising they would get no help from the other. Who would get the murderer first?

Ж

The perfectly clipped lawn threw a protective arm across the front of an expensive detached house that was screened by trees and commanding views over Burrator Reservoir. This was home to Caroline and Kevin Cory. Called Yennadon House, it boasted five bedrooms, three bathrooms, and elegant living rooms; beneath lay an underground garage and cellar, with a boiler-room.

    The Cory's were curled up on a large sofa, sharing wine. Drawn curtains and a homely fire created a situation for romance, but Caroline had no inclination towards sexual intercourse which she thought dirty. Caroline was telling Kevin about DI Steadwell and her questions to Selina. Kevin took special interest for something to feed Abi Cantrell, thinking 'I intend unlocking you Miss Cantrell, and that mouse Selina might provide the key.' At the same time Caroline thought ' I intend unlocking you Selina, and Inspector Steadwell had better not get in the way.'

Ж

A few miles away Selina Leigh is sitting up in bed. Her mind is wandering back to the farm when she was eight years old…

    *…it was 1943. Stinkface says a war is on, but how would she know? She never goes to Yelverton, to school or shops, not*

*even church. The only other person she sees is John Jackson – he comes all the time and the men smoke and drink whisky. Sometimes they call her down from bed to light cigars – he has spills beside the open fire and she must bring flame while they puff – like they couldn't light their own filthy cigars? Sometimes they talk dirty; she knows this instinctively even though there is no woman to set her an example. Stinkface beats her for the smallest mistake - tells her she is stupid and lazy like her mother and threatens her with the billhook with the hooked part pointing up, and smoke coming in clouds from his fat cigar. She and Jackson are both frightened of him.*

*Now she is in bed upstairs, a tiny miserable room lighted by a smoky oil lamp, with an iron bed and wallpaper so old the pattern is a memory. The corrugated roof bangs in the wind. Their boots stamp on the stairs and she knows Stinkface and Jackson are coming to laugh and torment her. They fill the room with their big grown-up bodies and cigar smoke, calling her a pathetic runt and telling tales about Dartmoor and the horrible beasts that walk after dark. She is petrified but can never run away…*

…Selina, an old lady of seventy, pulled the sheets over her head and silently cries.

# Chapter 13. Dewer

Tyres hissed on tarmac as the red bike appeared around the corner as Bill Merriweather pedalled determinedly in the morning sunshine.
Frank and Robin waved him down.
"Yelverton in the war must have been full of goings on," said Frank, "lots of babies born to airmen?"
Merriweather was silent, antagonistic.
"Miller is a Polish surname as well as an English one, but Stanislaw is definitely Polish. You do know Stanislaw Miller Bill, don't you?"
He nodded.
"His grandfather was Polish ground crew at Harrowbeer and knew the pilots well, so that's where he got the story about the gold, don't you think Bill?"
"P'raps."
"We've come from the Public Record Office," said Robin.
Merriweather stayed silent.
"No matter Bill," continued Frank, "but you are the man who knows Yelverton backwards – remember? Come and see you was the invitation. Heard of John Jackson, a handyman and thief? The records show your mother not as Jennifer Merriweather but Jennifer Jackson, so what happened?"
Merriweather was morose and deflated.
"Yes, John Jackson was my father for what he was worth. Mother said it was a mistake to marry him – something she

covered up when I was born. The parish records said a Flight Lieutenant Nigel Merriweather of RAF Harrowbeer had been killed in action. Although Merriweather was a total stranger to her, she told the registrar that he was the baby's father and that he'd intended their marriage on his return. There was a war on you know, so this was accepted. The name Merriweather would give me a better start than Jackson."

"What happened to John Jackson?" asked Frank.

"Disappeared."

"What about the gold?"

"Disappeared with him."

"I'll be frank Bill – you know lots about this gold don't you?"

"No."

He sullenly turned and continued cycling to the Cory residence. Robin said, "Did you notice his shoes and how they are worn down from his cycle pedals? Just like Mister Leeden's."

Ж

Another call from the mystery Vendor got under Brightwell's skin - all this cloak and dagger stuff was starting to irritate, and this made him blurt out, "It's only a matter of time before we discover your identity, so stop playing games and let's do business."

"O.K. Send your man to Plymouth Railway Station. I'll let you know the time and date. Same telephone kiosk." the Vendor answered.

Brightwell rang Weismann and told him this latest development.

"Simon, I am growing tired of all these non-productive comings and goings. I am here to do business and turn over money. You will be my new Envoy. Get instructions and go to Plymouth and wait at the telephone box. You will personally get this consignment and do not fail. If the Vendor was responsible for the body in the cave you will kill him. I'm sure you understand your fee will cover such a small thing – it has become a matter of principle with me."

Brightwell thought he was the go-between, not the errand boy and certainly not an assassin; things were spinning out of control - but for $3 million it was worth it.

Ж

Perfume and perspiration filled the motel bedroom, the muted TV flickering on scattered clothing: there a blouse and here a brassiere; trousers, shirt, skirt and panties; all hastily abandoned. Naked, a man and a woman lay entwined on crumpled sheets; he on his back, she propped on an elbow with her breasts exposed, and black lustrous hair tangled over her smooth shoulders and onto his broad chest; her flawless back stretching to the gentle swell of hip and buttocks. Abi and Kevin were in the afterglow of searching and hungry lovemaking. Abi fondled Kevin, and he, admiring her beauty, responded.

"Oh Kevin, where did you learn such things?"

He looked both manfully embarrassed and smug.
She thought him ready for subtle interrogation concerning a certain Mister Leeden.
"I always rely on your local knowledge Kevin, you being so well connected and admired. What have you found out about this body in the cave?"
"Well, I heard they're calling him Mister Leeden and the cops are struggling to find a name or anything about him."
"Heard anything about money - people say large sums could be involved?"
"Abi, if a lot of money was involved we would be in a hotel bedroom in Benidorm."
Abi thought, ' You must be joking Kevin, me being touted around smoke-filled rooms like a trophy? I may be a lot of things but I'm not a gangster's moll. Benidorm you bloody cheapskate? Not with you Kevin. I wouldn't go to Barbados with you."
"Kevin dear, have anything else to tell Abi?"
"There's a lot of police interest in an abandoned place called Leigh Farm on the disused railway track between Yelverton and the village of Princetown. It's not far from Leeden Tor."
"Think I'll look up there."
"Leave your car at Yelverton shops, cross Yennadon Down, and then up the old railroad - too many inquisitive people on the drivable rough track."
'Simple, Abi my girl', she silently congratulated herself.
Kevin found his second wind and pushed her off her elbow and back onto the bed.

Ж

Selina is in bed wondering why she is getting so much attention. It must be about Leigh Farm and the war years and...

*...Spring of 1944 when she was nine... how Jackson the Handyman comes to the farm telling tales of the pilots flying their planes away for 'something big' in the war. The aerodrome is deserted now and the pilots' house is under Jackson's control. He has dug up something worth a fortune and can prove it – Stinkface and Jackson go to his jeep and throw off a tarpaulin. She sidles up and can see a grey wooden box with writing on. The box has already been opened. They lift the lid and her father gasps. Inside is a block of gold, a thick slab of yellow with a bird and numbers stamped on it – Jackson says there is more but they are heavy and he can only manage one at a time up from the cellar, but they have all the time in the world with the Poles gone. Her father whispers something and Jackson says he will move it to that place as soon as it is dark. They drink whisky and smoke cigars and she has to wait on them and bring food.*
*After the men have eaten Jackson tells her father he will empty the house in a week and move everything to the hiding place.*

*Jackson has gone. Now it's just her and Stinkface, telling her she is useless. He bullies and terrifies her into silence – tells her she has not been baptised and God is not interested in her. How he frightens her with a story about Dewer the Devil who lives on Dartmoor, who rides a huge black horse at night and has claws like the billhook. How*

*Dewer lures people to their deaths over a pinnacle called the Dewerstone Rocks. How his dogs - phantom hounds that run the lonely moor at night - take the unbaptised down to Hell. They are called the Wisch Hounds, the Devil's horrible coal-black hunting dogs with eyes of red fire.*

*She is alone in her cold, miserable bedroom. Jackson said 'he would move the last of the gold to the hiding place' which is somewhere she does not know…not yet…*

Ж

Frank returned to Caroline Cory who greeted her, "Well if it's not our friend the rozzer come for her next Aphonia lesson." Frank saw Selina again, but nothing was learned from either woman until she was being shown out by Caroline.
"Selina was once given a pet by Merriweather – a rag-doll cat called Promise and she did take an interest in it."
"What happened to the kitten?"
"It died," said Caroline coldly.
She smiled a tight-lipped smile and turned away, leaving Frank to see herself out.

Frank saw Bill Merriweather talking to Matron Miller. Frank went straight up and brought a map from her handbag, asking them to point out Leigh Farm and wondering whether there was a road in? It was a very direct question which took them by surprise and they both looked uncomfortable and wary. This supplied Frank with another small piece of the jigsaw. She left and began driving to the Walkham Valley to see what remained of this Leigh Farm.

# Chapter 14. Leigh Farm

The yellow sailing jacket swished and her boots rubbed. Abi Cantrell had followed Kevin's advice - she didn't want to be seen by locals - so was going to approach Leigh Farm on foot across the moor. As advised she had left her car at Yelverton and walked Iron Mine Lane and Yennadon Down, and was now on the old railway track itself. The rails and sleepers had been removed long since, leaving a road of compressed chippings. Abi passed the concrete base of a workmen's hut with the remnants of a fireplace; a reminder of the track workers who had taken refreshments here; but they had all left more than a half-century ago. There were no other walkers or hikers - she had it all to herself. Dead bracken plastered the moorland, rust-red, flat and lifeless, and vestiges of snow still clung to leeward pockets of land. The going was fairly easy but during her journey she realised how remote the track was, with Leeden Tor looming as a jagged smear on the skyline away to her right. She knew Leigh was a hill-farm at the top of the Walkham Valley and beyond the enclosed fields but hadn't reckoned on the surroundings being quite so wild. Abi walked under a big sky, across which dark clouds scudded before a freshening wind. The old railroad gradually climbed away from the valley on her left, where the hedge-rimmed fields stretched out and upwards towards open moorland.

Astonished at the difference between the green of the fields and the dun of the wild moors, Abi was amazed when the sun shone on these prepared fields; at the vibrancy of their colours compared to the untamed Land above. The fields glowed with green tinged light and she gained the fanciful impression it was welling-up from the ground and not falling from the sky above. Cultivation had gradually given way to the uplands where the last of the hedges resembled humankind's efforts to tame their surroundings - to tie down the wildness with ropes of green hedges - their upper reaches marking the point where the valley farmers had run out of ropes, or perhaps will. Water chuckled in brooks and burbling through gullies, 'With an endless tinkling like tiny voices' thought Abi, surprising herself at her eloquence: but it all seemed so different up here. She'd been accompanied by the trill of birds flying in small colourful clouds but nothing else.

It was evident that the hand of progress was only in the track on which she walked, and also the hollowed-out Ingra Tor from where stonemasons had hewn granite. The brooding moor closed in on either side as she entered Dartmoor's wildness and she marvelled how the Landscape could be so open and yet so oppressive at the same time? There was neither person nor building, just rolling moorland and the empty railroad climbing on it snake-like progress to faraway Princetown. The old spoil-heaps of Swell Tor loomed way ahead on the horizon. Abi was all alone and lonely. An hour later and she found the remains of Leigh Farm on her left. This had taken longer than planned; it was late afternoon when she arrived and the sun was lowering towards the bastion-like Vixen Tor, far away westwards.

Enclosed with dry-stone walls and marked by scrubby, wind-blasted trees, was a square two story house with a red-rust corrugated iron roof and its front wall completely collapsed into what had passed as the garden. Even from a distance its dilapidation was manifest. Her first reaction was why any sane person would live on this utterly exposed wasteland where only sheep could scratch a living from tangled heather, peat, and course grasses. God knows how it must be in the middle of winter but Abi suspected God had already forsaken it. The sound of water splashing down the streams and brooks had lost all its earlier melody; now it played on her nerves and exaggerated her loneliness. The water-voices were whispering about her and laughing, mockingly. Overhead a buzzard wheeled and gave its mewling cry and Abi had the feeling of being watched from the house by something cat-sly and silent. An atmosphere of malignance hung over the place - a sense of guarding wickedness, made worse by the sibilance of running water and the sighing of the wind. Leigh Farm seemed to observe her – to *know* her. Abi had the distinct feeling of not being wanted – that the house was shunning her presence – and this unnerved her; she shuddered at her vulnerability. Then she noticed that someone had been digging holes around the house and garden; some pits were obviously historic but others very recent indeed. Presented with the unsubtle clue that something had been hidden and badly wanted she wondered if this was tied to Mister Leeden or Selina.

She stopped, hands on hips, bewildered how something so ruined could still stand. The farm had been built from rough stones picked up within walking distance and arranged into this gaunt pile. A two-up-two-down, with outbuildings for a washhouse and a rudimentary lavatory. The front had completely collapsed, exposing the interior in the manner of a mad person's doll's house. Rusted corrugated-iron jutted from the roof which was rattled and bumped by the wind, and ceiling timbers protruded, finger-like, blindly seeking support from the long-gone front wall. Profusions of small ferns grew over the floors and the house had been colonised by lichens. Inside and out it was green with mildew: a mournful excuse of a habitation. Negotiating the front garden confirmed the place a chaotic mess. Apart from piles of fallen masonry the garden was randomly strewn with broken crockery, a smashed picture frame, and the rusted remains of canned food. Incongruously, there lay a coffee mug containing the image of a matelot with a pretty girl on his arm and 'Kiss Me Quick – A Present from Paignton.' Her skin crawled at the voyeurism in looking at other people's possessions, and although they were long departed from this place she realised, nonetheless, that she was an intruder. The collapse had presented the house's interior to the elements and she looked into a ground level kitchen on one side and a living room with a fireplace on the other. There were numerous holes in the downstairs floors all uniform in shape; long on one side and narrow on the other. The whole ground floor was a death-trap and she turned her attention upwards. Deciding to have a poke around the upper floor of this crazy doll's house she crept very carefully up the slippery, creaking stairs. A wooden staircase climbed to a small landing and two bedrooms, one left and the other right: that was the sum total of Leigh Farm.

Abi had just entered the room on her left and saw it contained a cot-like bed of tubular iron, with exposed springs. Then she froze – there was an undulating note gathering strength – a motor sounded in the distance: someone was coming. She hissed "Company at a time like this. Get hidden girl." She clattered down the green stairs and scrambled outside to crouch behind a dry-stone wall. From there she peered through a gap to see who her disturber was.

Ж

Frank Steadwell was stoically gripping her steering wheel – saloon cars were made for main roads not jolting on un-surfaced tracks - when she saw the remains of Leigh Farm in the distance. Her instincts told her something was waiting here that would prove vital in her understanding of Selina and the whole case. The track ended and she walked the final two hundred yards. There was still daylight but it would be gone in thirty minutes. She strode out, noting dry-stone walls and stunted trees, rough pasture and natural water; all things to which she was accustomed both as a county police officer and farmer's daughter. Nonetheless, it was a marvel that people worked such land; not that anyone had worked this place since 1947 according to the retired PC Dennis.

Frank took stock of the house: Len Dennis's warning that it was perilously derelict was correct. She was unaware of being watched by Abi Cantrell who was hiding thirty yards away. To Frank's eyes the open-fronted house resembled a butcher's carcass – one cut apart and dressed out - the house was the empty cavity and the exposed stubs of flooring and roofing timbers resembled truncated, saw-through ribs. Like Cantrell she detected an atmosphere coming from the house, not of rejection but one of pure evil and spite; to her it represented raw harm and suffering and like Cantrell she felt unwanted. This made her determined to press on. She negotiated the wanton tangle of the front garden before carefully mounting the stairs to the landing where she entered a bedroom – this time on the right. It had a small window devoid of glass that looked out towards Swell Tor, and it contained a rusted double bed with mouldering mattress. On a sideboard stood a grimy wash-basin and a rusted cut-throat razor: obviously a man's room. The only other bedroom had its door pushed back hard against the rear wall and it housed a single cot of iron. Frank kept away from the empty space on her left, the space where the front of the house had once been, still unaware that she was being closely watched by Cantrell. Crossing the bedroom to the far window she noted the faded remains of ragged curtains, and walls covered in a blue print wallpaper that was almost transparent with age. On the window-sill stood a pathetic link with the past, a cheap glazed jug from which protruded the dry and skeletal remains of a bunch of wild flowers. The attempt to brighten this drab little cell touched her very core and Frank's heart went out to the room's erstwhile female occupant – to Selina – and with tears in her eyes she made a promise to do her best for the old lady. She thought of her own children and their clean and bright bedrooms with drawings and posters bedecking the walls - thought of her thirteen year old Alice who still held onto girlish innocence in the cosy world of her own bedroom, and Frank seethed at the injustice that had reigned here. Then instinct told her to look behind the door. It had been pushed hard back against the rear bedroom wall and had stuck in this position to form a concealed triangular space - probably the driest and least exposed place in the whole house - and she tugged this door free from the swollen floorboards. Fixed behind the door was a piece of brittle drawing paper about two feet square and pinned in place with thumb tacks. Filling the door's upper half the paper was yellow with age and curling at the corners. Frank stared open-mouthed with shock as she absorbed a crude image. Roughly drawn but full of primitive energy she was looking at a crayon drawing of a devil-like man. He was accompanied by a black dog whose face peered malevolently at the viewer from around the devilman's waist. They stared balefully and formed a chilling pair. Both had long claws closely resembling the bill-hook favoured by farmers and these had been coloured blood-red. What disturbed Frank most were the eyes of devilman and his dog and she shuddered with loathing. Both had been burned out to glaring empty holes – burned by a cigarette, or judging by their size by a fat cigar – and burned from the back through to the front where the singed and ragged edges stood out in a parody of dark eyelashes.  Scrawled across the bottom in an untidy hand, was the single word **DEWER**.

   Frank tugged the paper free, her mind making rapid connections with the drawings she had seen in Selina's room, when the bullet smacked into the wall inches from her head. It left a hole the diameter of a pencil. They say you never hear the bullet that kills you and she would agree with that sentiment to the end of her days – there had been no crack from the rifle or whine of the incoming round - and rifle it must have been to have that degree of accuracy at the distance from which someone was shooting.  These thoughts went through Frank's mind in the slow-motion of a millisecond until a voice inside her head said, quite levelly, 'Someone is trying to kill you.' This galvanised her and she dodged behind the door, pulling it to. The next bullet splintered wood from the doors edge and buried itself into the wall, spraying her with soft plaster like mouldy cheese. Still clutching the drawing she pushed the door back and scattered down and out as fast as she dared.  Another round thwacked into one of the wooden stairs beside her foot. Outside she searched desperately for a hiding place and found one behind a boulder in the disorderly front garden. Peeking over she saw the setting sun glint from something up in the region of Leeden Tor – like light reflecting off glass – followed by a flash as a rifle was fired again and another round clanged off the corrugated roof. Frank got down as small as she could. A zipping sound heralded a fifth bullet that slammed into an old lorry gearbox, where it disintegrated in a spray of sluggish oil and cast iron splinters. Then the shooter turned their attention on Abi Cantrell in her yellow jacket, who was hiding the wrong side of the stone wall and completely exposed in the large white circle of a telescopic sight. Squeezing the trigger, the shooter slammed a bullet into the wall inches from Abi's waist and another towards her exposed head – it pinged off the top of the wall and wailed its exit from the scene. Another ploughed into the grass about six feet from one of her boots, showering her with grit. Cantrell thought 'Blow this for a game of soldiers, I'm off.' She did so at a scuttling run ending twenty yards later as she jumped down into a freezing cold brook where she sat waist-deep in peat-stained water. A bird eyed her curiously and she said, "What are you staring at you ugly so-and-so?" The bird flew off but she stayed safe, chaffing herself for not finding whatever Steadwell had retrieved from behind the door. She consoled herself, "Your black luck, Abi."

The setting sun was full in the shooter's eyes: five uncomfortable minutes and ten more poorly aimed bullets passed before the dearth of sunlight signalled the ordeal was over. The shooter had pocketed the empty cartridge cases and left the vantage point long before either women thought it safe to peek. Frank, still oblivious to Cantrell's presence, regained the sanctuary of her car and drove away as fast as she dared with the drawing on the seat beside her - viewing it with the pride a hunter might give a trophy. Now she knew what had happened in that farmhouse; Selina had been the victim of psychological child abuse by her father, and probably physical abuse for good measure. She believed Professor Cory already knew this but had said nothing, and Frank wondered why? The cold and grumbling Abi, relieved that she had thought to bring a torch in her pocket, squelched her way back down the pitch-dark railroad and across a windswept Yennadon Down. She arrived at her car shortly before nine: wet, hungry, and empty-handed.

# Chapter 15. Some Dartmoor Legends

The following morning Frank was again having tea with Len Dennis. He seemed to relish the attention much more than his daughter, but Frank got her way and was seeing him alone. "Len, tell me about the Dartmoor legends please?"

"The history of Dartmoor pre-dates history itself and has been passed down by word-of-mouth in moorland pubs, and when moorland families sat around their fireplaces during the long winter's nights. Dartmoor is a wilderness full of wonderful but dangerous things and must be taken seriously - and many a fool has paid a price for laughing at that bit of advice - so let's start with Childe's Tomb. Childe was his family name and he was a hunter on horseback who was on the moor returning from a hunting trip when caught in a massive blizzard. He pistolled and disembowelled the horse and climbed inside the cavity and that's how they found them, frozen together in death. There is a stone cross to him near Foxtor Mires and some say his spirit still rides on snowy nights. Foxtor Mires, and there is another place not to go alone for it is an unforgiving bog into which lost travellers have been swallowed. Then Jay's Grave where a woman - she was a poor workhouse apprentice who hanged herself - is buried away from any church as was the custom with suicides in those times: well, fresh flowers are regularly found on her grave but no-one ever admits placing them – and this has been happening for two centuries or more. There are stories of marsh ghosts and pixies and a pair of hairy hands that appear and menace people. Think of all the Stone Age burial mounds up there and what secrets they may contain. Cloven Devil footprints appeared in 1855, and this story is well documented: following overnight snow a single set of hoof prints was found, visible prints which went over fields and rivers and over the tops of houses. They were reported all over by various people from Dartmoor into South Devon and then the next county of Dorset and stretched up to one hundred miles. If you don't believe me look it up."

Len was getting into his stride. "So, it's easy for modern folk to scoff at the olden days and the people who spun those yarns - we who have electricity and telephones and the Internet, we have good roads and cars with headlights and heaters and a radio. If you tell young people today to connect with nature they end up staring at a tiny bright screen in the palm of their hand. Back then the people had nothing, no protection, no police force to turn to, and had to rely on their own efforts. At night the moorland people got inside their houses and they bolted the doors and shuttered the windows. Sitting around a blazing fire and telling their tales was a way of reminding them how secure and happy they were. But it was a brittle happiness and the driving rain that rattled the house made them fearful, or dogs howling in the distance, or great drifts of snow piling up into their porchway and imprisoning them for days or weeks on end. They were riddled with superstition and believed such things were sent to punish them, that any bad thing was retribution for something wicked they had done and their sins were sure to find them out. They lived in tiny inward-looking societies. Modern folk make fun of such things but many a time I have been on the moor at night and it can be very lonely and frightening up there on your own – especially hearing the long drawn-out howl of an unseen dog, or the grass rustling and there is no wind, or you are convinced a shadow is following in your footsteps. Only a fool laughs at something they can't understand."

Frank was not laughing when she opened her briefcase and withdrew the drawing from Selina's old bedroom at Leigh Farm. She gently placed it in Len's lap and sat back. He sat forward and stared silently at the paper and the scrawled word **DEWER** before speaking again, "The Devil and one of his Wisch Hounds – Dewer is Celtic for the Devil you know - but I have never seen the eyes removed in such a way. Burned through into round holes; how strange and whatever does that mean? About three miles from Yelverton is The Dewerstone – a series of rock pinnacles that rise out of the wooded valley of the River Plym – and the highest peak stands at one hundred and sixty feet. Legend says Dewer waits for dark nights and lures lost travellers over the rocks to their deaths."

Frank told him how and where she got it and he said "He must have burned out those eyes. I wouldn't put anything past that bully – Harold Leigh was a scoundrel and a villain - please

don't show that to Selina? She's suffered enough and Harold Leigh still casts a long shadow over her."
"Were you sorry when the wall fell on him, Len?"
"No Inspector I was not sorry at all. I would not have wished any man dead but I was pleased to be rid of him – and not only because he was the author of all my crime but also for the people he was corrupting: that man had already ruined a lot of lives and there are times when the bad apple can spoil the whole damned barrel 'scusing my French ma'am. He died unlamented by me or any I know and is buried in the graveyard at Walkhampton Church. Best place for the bugger, I say."

Frank thanked the old man and left. When alone Len mused about something he had not mentioned, the legend of Crazywell Pool, a natural and deep water feature situated in a desolate place and fairly close to Leeden Tor. The tale told of a residing gnome, a spirit that could reveal the names of those about to die in the coming year. Len Dennis recited the old saying to himself, wondering if that infernal Polish gold would claim any lives before this matter was finished…

'A spirit neither malignant nor benign dwelt at Crazywell,
A Nether-Gnome from whom was not hidden the future of men.'
Unlike the Nether-Gnome, Len did not know. He hoped none would die but suspected otherwise. It was as well the future was hidden from Len because deaths were going to follow, and not too far in the future - not too far at all.

Ж

Wood-fire shone amber through glasses; soft music played and customers polite conversation was occasionally pierced by the ringing of the cash register. Robin drank beer, happy in his favourite pub, one of the only ones that he was happy to visit. Then came the voluptuous Abi Cantrell, hips swinging, red dress swishing, black hair tumbling, carrying a hat-box by its braided rope and a rain-drenched coat over her arm. Abi knew Robin took a taxi home at eight.
She was still seething inwardly over Robin's flight from her attentions; men should never resist her charms so she'd decided to take him prisoner and divest him of his innocence, followed by the delicious irony of interviewing a dazed detective.
Perfume wafted as she slid beside him, flashing her stockinged thigh and placing a hand on his arm.
   "Be a sweetie Robin and buy me a gin and tonic? Ice, no slice."
He stuttered, staring down her low-cut top, and then went and returned with the drink. She patted, "Thanks, sit here love." Alone again with Abi the Diva he was mesmerised into submission.
"What awful rain - April showers and all that? Well Robin fancy bumping into you; come here often? I'm going home to coq au vin, but popped in for a quickie. How about you?" She sipped, watching his child-like wariness.
"Same here Abi, I have a taxi in ten minutes."

She feigned surprise, "What luck, I can share the cab if you drop me off first. My cottage is only a mile outside town. Good, I'm pleased that's settled. Drink up dear, we've time for another." The rabbit meekly obeyed the fox. It was that easy.

Rain sluiced the taxi's windscreen as headlights picked out Abi's isolated cottage. "Oh Robin, be a love and carry my hatbox to the door?"

He pinched the rope between finger and thumb, jiggling the empty box, "Not heavy, is it?"

Abi smiled dazzlingly, "Fascinators weigh almost nothing." Robin dashed through pelting rain and looked back. Abi was running - the taxi paid off and pulling away. Robin put up a finger and squeaked, but too late; he'd been abducted. They entered a kitchen with no sign or smell of casserole. Her stilettos tapped flagstones and she sashayed, silkily, into a comfortable sitting room where soft furniture was scattered with bright cushions. She lighted a table lamp, dimly. "You're all wet Robin. Give me your jacket and pop into the bedroom to dry – it's on the left. I'll fix drinks."

He closed the bedroom door and cast about for an escape route, his phone and jacket already gone. Her knock startled him, "Robin, your wet trousers and socks. Be a honey and pass them out." He complied then returned, bare-legged, damp-shirted and tousled-haired. Tinkling ice cracked in glasses of gin and tonic, there was low music, but no Abi. She called, "Get comfy while I change."

Robin looked in vain for his things. Abi returned wearing a frothy lilac negligée which displayed her fabulous figure.

Passing him a gin and tonic she indicated the spacious sofa. He sought refuge in a single armchair so she perched on the arm. Gulping gin, Robin made to stand but she blocked his way. The negligée parted and he fell back. Angling her naked body she pushed forward bare breasts,
"What do you think of these?"
Believing flippancy would save the day he quipped,
"Like a photo-finish in a Zeppelin race?"
He stood no chance; she threw a leg over him and stifled his protests with her ample mouth. Before Detective Sergeant Robin Allenby could say "Arrestable Offence" she had taken him into her own sweet custody.

Ж

...*it is 1945 and Selina is ten. Jackson and Stinkface talk about the war ending and the Poles coming back, then Jackson talks about the stash. Her father takes Selina in his truck to a secret tunnel with a metal door, hidden inside a hill. She hears them say Burrator. Jackson has reversed his jeep inside. Her father speaks.*
"Have you got all of the gold out of Storm Haven?"
"Yes."
*Jackson points to the end of the tunnel where wooden boxes are stacked. There are a lot of boxes, grey in colour with a strange black bird on the side. One of these boxes has been opened and four gold ingots sit on the lid. Again they have that funny bird on them, and some letters. His cigar is perched on the edge of the box and a column of smoke drifts.*

"Have you repaired the cellar floor at Storm Haven?"
"Harold, no one would know."
"Tell anyone?"
"'Course not"
"Anyone know you were coming here, or seen you?"
"No."
"Is that top box unsteady?"
Jackson turns and looks. Her father grabs Jackson's hair in one hand and cuts his throat with the billhook. Jackson thrashes but her father holds onto him. He dies and is thrown aside.
"Keep silent Selina or you will go to Hell. Dewer's claw is like the billhook and that is what will happen to you, little girl." She has to help her father prop Jackson's body behind the steering-wheel of his jeep.

Later, when they were back on the farm, she in her bed and he towering over her Harold Leigh was holding up drawing to Selina.

**DEWER** had been scrawled at the bottom of the drawing which was of a devil and his dog.
"If you ever speak about the gold or Jackson, Dewer the Devil will take you down to Hell and burn you. See how Dewer's eyes are blood red?" With his cigar he burns the eyes out of the devil and his dog, from back through to front, the smoke swirling from ragged holes.
"See how their eyes glow?"
Holding her wrist in an iron grip he puffs his cigar to bright red, poking it through the eye socket and burning her arm with the tip."
Selina thrashes and screams.

*"That's how it will be in Hell."*
*Harold Leigh pins the drawing to her bedroom door.*
*"Dewer will always watch you with those black eyes even when I'm not here, even when you're asleep - God is not interested in children who've not been baptised, only Dewer is." Selina sobs herself to sleep, worried what will happen when she dies?*

# Chapter 16.  Death, Certified

"Selina is dying" said Caroline, and Matron nodded.  Midday sun shone on Selina's bed, on her lethargic state and difficult breathing.
"This is a final decline from which nothing can save her – not even me."
Matron accepted this unquestioningly, without qualm.
"You will find her tomorrow – she will have died in her sleep - I will certify her when I arrive.  I'm taking a half-day off and do not expect to be disturbed."
Matron sniffed as she watched Caroline's Range Rover driven away.

Ж

"Plymouth – off for Plymouth" called the train manager.  It was five-thirty pm, on a bright day.  Simon Brightwell, the new Envoy, had been contacted by the Vendor and given instructions that would lead to a face-to-face meeting. He was dressed in casual green jacket and grey trousers - the last thing he intended was to dress at all like Mister Leeden -  thinking that one can never be too careful about what sets others off. Neither was he carrying a briefcase, only a handy-jotter and pen in his jacket pocket. He went to the agreed telephone kiosk and waited, and after a few minutes the phone rang and he picked up.

"A very indistinct voice, very muffled as though the speaker was talking through a handkerchief, spoke.
"Go to the bus stop outside the University in Tavistock Road. Catch the bus to Yelverton and get off. There is a Portuguese cafe in the row of shows. Wait there. What is your mobile number?"
He gave it, and the voice said, "There is a timetable and map wedged behind the kiosk, where the power supply comes in."
The call ended.
Brightwell left the kiosk and quickly found the map. He was close to the bus stop and, following the Vendor's directions he waited. Brightwell would be pleased when this was finished and he could sever all links with Weismann.
'This started as a gold deal and now I'm supposed to murder the vendor. This gold has taken on a life of its own.' He felt uncomfortable and out of his depths.

    The bus arrived and he boarded for Yelverton. The journey took him through the cities northern suburbs where the bus left the limits and entered Dartmoor National Park. Brightwell was astonished how quickly he'd gone from a built-up area to wide open spaces. They crossed a wild expanse of heath which the map told him was Roborough Down, with the heights of Dartmoor smudge in the distance. Wild ponies, cattle, and sheep, freely grazed. There was still daylight but it would be gone in an hour or so, and he wondered where he would spend the night?

At Yelverton the bus stopped at a waiting area. Kevin Cory stayed on the bus, from where he'd had Brightwell under close observation - but Brightwell got off and walked the few steps to the café. An attractive young woman was coming out and Brightwell held open the door. The smell of fresh coffee mixed with her perfume, they smiled, she insinuated her way past and then shot a backward glance. Had they spoken they would have recognised each other's voice from all their telephone calls, but neither did and she was there by sheer coincidence. Once Brightwell was inside and Abi had driven away, Kevin Cory got off and the bus and into his black Jaguar car which was parked close to the cafe door. He intended to be sure Brightwell was alone before revealing his identity.
Simon Brightwell and Abi Cantrell had passed like ships in the night: this was as well because Kowalski's people had seen the semi-interplay from the camper van.

Brightwell ordered coffee and a Portuguese custard tart and settled down.

Ж

Caroline arrived home with the makings of dinner for three, hefting plastic bags onto the kitchen's granite worktop. Kevin was on an errand and Bill was in the basement working on the gas boiler. She went down the interior stairs, swinging her hip around Bill's cycle.

"The big rifle needs a good clean Caroline. I'll put it back in the cabinet when I have finished, being careful not to touch the settings on the telescopic sight."
"Bill, will you have a look at the Range Rover - it sounds a bit lumpy."
"Sure Caroline – shall I have a quick drive while you prepare dinner?"
"Good idea Bill." She returned with car keys and a mug of coffee.
Bill sipped, confident of being repaid with a meal.

Ж

"If Caroline can have time off so can I", thought Marion Miller. She pulled up outside Storm Haven and went downstairs with sandwiches and coffee. Strip-lighting flooded the cellar, casting crazy shadows amongst the forest of scaffolding. Stan was seated in the centre of this criss-cross of shade and light, engrossed in cleaning his hunting rifle and polishing the telescopic sight. He looked up.
"Those enforcers were back." The light illuminated the split lip and swollen eye. "They've threatened to kill me and they mean it."
He angrily thumbed fat cartridges into the magazine and she ran and knelt at his side, producing an envelope stuffed with money.
"No need for more violence Stan. Look, this should buy then off until we find the gold."

"Where did you get this money - how much is here?"
"Five thousand pounds. It's a loan from Caroline."
"I didn't know she had it in her. Fancy that - Caroline the Good Samaritan?"
"Have some food Stan. Your Polish grandfather was ground crew and he swore the gold was hidden in this very house. It has to be buried in the cellar Stan because there's nowhere else to hide it."
They ate in silence as spills of dust floated down. Marion alone with the thought that Selina would soon be dead and the secret would die with her. She was frightened to mention it to Stan. Best say nothing and keep digging.

Ж

The nurse rinsed her hands and water gurgled down the plughole - its sound taking the semi-conscious Selina back to another time and place…

*Water gurgled through the dry stone wall – there had been heavy rain and the garden at Leigh Farm was saturated. "Selina, get the other side and push through the gaps with this stick. I'll scrape down here with the billhook." Her feet were cold and water squelched in her shoes but she pushed and poked while he complained on the other side. Then the wall leaned slightly and she stood on tiptoe and looked over. Head down, he was swearing through a fog of cigar smoke and hadn't noticed. The wall heeled a little farther and never came back - nothing critical but certainly out of vertical. His scrapings were taking out small parts of the base – each making it tilt a little more over his bent back – but he still hadn't noticed. She pushed lightly and was astonished how finely balanced it was – she, a thirteen year old girl could move a wall one-handed. "You're as useless as your mother – push Selina or I'll get Dewar for you." She did and the wall balanced and then started to topple in slow-motion. 'Fall' she whispered flinging her weight against it. Stones scraped dryly as the wall toppled and a huge section fell on him. The ground shook and she leapt through the breach onto a pile of loose rocks. At first she thought he'd scurried away but he'd managed to turn before the stones got him. Pinned and buried face-down, his legs and left arm were covered with stones and a heap rested on his broad back. His right arm was twisted and crooked-up beside his face. Unconscious, he'd instinctively clung to the billhook and the lighted cigar was clamped in his mouth. Selina plucked the cigar and pushed it into the tender flesh of his inner forearm. It spluttered and hissed and he murmured as she pushed harder. It sucked as she pulled it out, leaving a smoking black hole like Dewer's eye; she flung the cigar aside. Blood was dripping from his mouth and he was a grey colour. She knelt listening for breath but there was nothing - no more blood and he'd stopped breathing – he was dead and she was free. Selina began her long walk to Yelverton to find the Constable and tell what she'd done…*

Ж

Bill polished the telescopic sight on the chunky rifle, handling it with practised ease. Then he tiptoed to the basement stairs and listened up into the house. Caroline was busy in the kitchen and he got into the Range Rover and drove off. She smiled, drying her hands fussily with snow-white disposable towelling. Her watch said five-thirty pm, and there was something she had to do before cooking dinner.

# Chapter 17. A Penitence of Confessions

Bill drove less than a mile from the Cory's House to Burrator Reservoir, where he turned onto a rough track and then a small muddy trail. He reversed through bushes where the Range Rover was swallowed by greenery and then stopped beside rusty double doors. They were marked *Dynamite Store - Keep Out*. The doors were set into a wild, overgrown hillside. Bill had found the doors long ago but now he could get inside. He'd waited a long time for this moment and with trembling hands he selected a small brass key from the Range Rover's keyring and unfastened the padlock. The bolt scraped and put his teeth on edge. First one and then the second, the double doors creaked as he dragged them open. There was a release of unpleasant air as his torchlight illuminated a windowless concrete tunnel which housed a canvassed-topped World War II jeep, and rows of neatly stacked boxes. A foetid smell persisted and he experienced a feeling of foreboding. Skirting the jeep he stood beside grey boxes stencilled with an eagle and the words, "Aircraft Parts. Property of Free Polish Airforce." One was open and he knew, before he looked, what it contained: Bill flipped aside an old blanket and gazed in awe at the four gold ingots. He noticed that one of the bars had had a corner hacksawn off. Each was stamped with a Polish eagle - a serial number - and 12.5 kg. He beheld the treasure of Storm Haven. "So it was true, mother." he said aloud to himself.

His joy was interrupted by the whiff of foulness - an unwholesomeness coming from the jeep - like something had been spilled and not properly cleaned up. Peering inside he saw a pile of old clothes that morphed into a nightmare; a ghoul from some perverted movie was sitting behind the steering wheel. His heart pounded in his throat and his skin crawled. Bill was being grinned at by a long dead body, yet grin did no justice to this rictus; it was the grimace of a soul that had died in agony. Shaking his head was futile - he could not shake the image off - the corpse resembled an Egyptian Mummy unwound after three thousand years in a pyramid. Skin like badly dried jerky stretched across the skeletal face. The throat had been cut through in a long jagged slash, with remnants of a red neckerchief clinging to the ancient wound. A scruffy jacket clothed the erstwhile driver whose twig-like bones protruding from scuffed cuffs. Bill Merriweather was looking at the earthly remains of his long dead father. Then Bill's head swam and a black hole rushed up from the floor and engulfed him…

*…he was staring into the shapes formed by the red-hot coals and imaged a castle, or was it a big monster? Bill was sitting in a tin bath of warm, soapy water, in front of a kitchen range - the oven door was open and warmth washed him, inside and out. His mother hummed as she worked at her sink, occasionally sparing a loving glimpse for her one-and-only child, her darling little Billy. A towel and pyjamas were draped over a kitchen chair and a book lay on the table. After his bed-time story his mother would ask him his favourite question "Do you want to know about the gold, Bill…?*

..."Do you want to know about the gold, Bill?
His mother kept asking but she had Caroline's face and voice. And then he snapped out of it. Bill was in the passenger seat of the jeep and handcuffed to its steering wheel. Looking right he saw the remains of John Jackson – then he looked left and Caroline Cory was swinging her Range Rover keys around one finger.

"I won't be keeping the handcuff key - won't need it again. Nice bike Bill but the seat is too narrow for me – still it got me here where I knew I would find you. You've been spying on Kevin and me for quite a while, and spying on my patient notes concerning Salina; you will have found the map of Burrator with its circles and notes and it was obvious you would check out this place and eventually find the steel door. The makers name on the padlock matched the key on my keyring so it was only a matter of time before you asked to borrow my Range Rover. So, transport here and the means to enter, all in one. Oh Bill, it was so easy - I placed the idea in your mind about the Range Rover being lumpy and, lo and behold, and you took the bait."

"What happened to me?"

"You just passed out Bill, because I poisoned the coffee you had at my house. I judged it to perfection and gave you enough time to get here before it worked its magic. Now check your left forearm and see the pinprick from the injection I gave a moment ago, while you were still unconscious."

He did and saw the speck of blood.

"I have given you a neuromuscular-inhibiting drug which will affect your spontaneous ventilation. The muscles in your throat will shut down and you will slowly asphyxiate and be dead in a few hours. That's why I won't need the handcuff key. Now, do you want to know about the gold, Bill?"

"There's nothing I would like better."

"The story about the horde had been going around for years so Kevin and I decided to investigate – Kevin followed rumours about Harold Leigh and John Jackson and I worked on Selina. She was always the key to unlock the gold which is why I took her on as a project - the milk of human kindness does not flow through my veins and I only brought her under my protection to get something in return. Selina had been pushed from one institution to another and was in a dead-end so I pretended to have an interest in her. She does not suffer from Aphonia and the problem lies in her mind. So what is your interest in the gold?"

"I wanted money to make her life better."

"How pathetic – a janitor with a heart."

"I pity her and that's why I bought her the kitten."

"Smelly bag of bacteria - a verminous distraction - did you think you could come between me and my patient with a cheap trick? That's why I poisoned it. "

Bill exploded with anger, thrashing and wrenching the steering wheel.

"Stop or I will shatter your thigh." Her voice carried its usual coldness but with extra confidence. She was pointing a business-like pistol at him. It was the semi-automatic previously owned by Mister Leeden and the barrel's black circle looked as large as the tunnel he was a prisoner in. Reluctantly Bill sat still and listened – the episode had tired him and he could not catch his breath – neither did he relish the thought of receiving a big and heavy bullet.

"Selina communicated through drawing books and that is where she made her slip. Recently she drew a devil figure accompanied by a large, awful dog. She is illiterate but does know some letters and numbers so I bullied her into scrawling the devil's name – it was Dewer – she had drawn Dewer and the Wisch Hound. Eureka! She was in the palm of my hand and could be frightened whenever I wanted – which I frequently did – telling her she would go to Hell if she did not draw what I wanted.  She drew a picture of a big door on a tunnel with the letters **Dymit** - her puerile spelling you know - and another drawing of a lake with a dam. Meanwhile, Kevin tied the gold at Storm Haven to Harold Leigh via the thief John Jackson; I assume he is that object beside you."

"Yes. I never met him but he happens to be my long-lost father."

"More confessions? The janitor son of a tuppence ha'penny handyman – and you thought you could outwit *me*?"

"How did you find this place?"

"An old map showing the explosive magazine at Burrator. We found the doors, sawed the lock, and the gold was ours. Then we put it back under our lock and key - the key you spied on the Range Rover's keyring."

"What are you going to do with the gold?"
"Kevin has found a disreputable gold dealer called Simon Brightwell – it takes one to know one, you know. Brightwell sent an Envoy to buy the gold but he offered only half its value – can you imagine? I have my principles, you know."
"What about this earlier Envoy?"
"We invited him to dinner at our house one evening before Christmas. Once we turned down his offer he became more demanding. I know people's minds and realised he was a killer. This gun was under his coat; he had come to steal the gold and kill us – so I got in early."
"How?"
"We suggested eating and then going back to the negotiations. He watched like a hawk and we had to eat a bit of everything before he did, but he wasn't as clever as me because I had painted clear poisoned onto his dessert spoon, and when he went under I gave him the fatal jab. He deserved death, he was an assassin and had this horrible gun and poisons in his pocket. We were stuck with his body so I stretched him out and closed his eyes and mouth, nice and neat. I like neatness. We kept him in our boiler room for a week while planning his disposal.
"What poisons?"
"Cyanide hidden inside cold remedy capsules; also Laburnum seeds – they contain Cytosine, a quinolizidine alkaloid which causes nausea and vomiting - high doses produce sleepiness, convulsions, coma, and frothing at the mouth, and extreme doses have been fatal. He was a poisoner all right."
"It takes one to know one, you know."

She arched an eyebrow but he continued.

"How did you get rid of him, Caroline?"

"He was carrying little; no driving licence or keys, no ID. Perhaps he had a left- luggage locker with a combination lock. We decided to leave his body on Dartmoor but he was wearing a grey lounge suit and tie and people don't wear that sort of thing up there. We burned his clothes in our basement and bought replacements from charity shops, mostly in Plymouth. I used an old pair of your shoes Bill, all worn down from cycling. There was a tattoo in his armpit – one of those Special Forces numbers - bleach and a dollop of battery acid saw to that. We hoped he'd be scattered by foxes but just to be safe we dressed him in an old jacket and woollen hat to make him look like a hiker. The poisons went back in his pockets to make it appear like suicide – he already had poison in his stomach from my meal, didn't he?

"Where did you dump him?"

"We chose Leeden Tor because it's close to our house, and I borrowed the rescue stretcher on the pretext of giving a lecture to a volunteer group. After dressing him and strapping his body into the stretcher we took him in the Range Rover and parked as close as we could, then dragged the stretcher across the moor at two in the morning. His shoes – your shoes Bill – kept coming off so we removed them and the socks until we got to the tor. His heels got battered but what the hell? I laid him out in the cave and left him tidy; I hate untidiness. The blizzards were unforeseen and he was snowed in and preserved. I had hoped that foxes would have scavenged him long before now."

"Who was he?

"He's a complete mystery, a total enigma. Perhaps Simon Brightwell can shed some light this evening; he's coming to dinner in a short while to make a second bid for the gold. If he won't offer the right price I shall poison him too; can't let him off if he knows where we live, can I Bill? If I poison Brightwell then Kevin can go at the same time because he's becoming a drag. Kevin cannot resist a certain type of woman because a hungry dog will eat dirty meat. He has another at the moment, that Abi Cantrell tart who is asking him too many questions about the body on Leeden Tor. He set her up to go to Leigh Farm with the intention of shooting her dead and, most conveniently, Inspector Frances Steadwell wandered along. Kevin being Kevin tried 'buy-one-get-one-free' and dismally got neither, but thanks for cleaning his rifle Bill. If I put Kevin out of his misery I shall report him missing and suggest he has gone off for a dirty weekend in Bournemouth or Brighton or some such place."

"Then what?

"I will buy a detached house with a very large garage and move one ingot at a time. The gold won't be going to Yennadon House; I'm not stupid and won't have it at home. After that I shall find someone who receives stolen goods – they call them a fence in the films, I do believe. Selina is dying. I have written and signed her death certificate and left it on the desk in my locked office: tomorrow I will fill in the time and date. I

poisoned her tea this morning and she will die in the early hours of tomorrow when I shall be at home in bed. There will be no post-mortem examination because I will certify her death, and who could challenge my eminence?"
"Why kill her?"
"She has passed usefulness both to me and the nursing home – is becoming more dependent and will cost more to keep; also, she had never given me the kudos that I deserve, has never spoken a single word and is most unlikely to recite poetry in front of an assembly of my medical peers. Selina was a promising project with a disappointing end. I resent her so she must go, so I destroyed all her medical notes and references to this place two hours ago. Very soon no part of her or her past, will exist."
"What about Marion?"
"Matron Miller has been complicit many times when troublesome patients have been put to sleep – she wants an easy life too. We have agreed that she will come early tomorrow and be the one to find Selina dead. The death certificate sitting on my desk is accompanied by the business card of a local undertaker. Acting as her 'next-of-kin' I shall request cremation: everything neat and tidy."
Bill stared with utter loathing at this dangerous woman. She was either an icy-cold fish or completely mad, but he was finished whatever. Breathing with difficulty he realised he was going to die alone in this horrible tunnel.

"So, I'm off to make dinner for Brightwell" she said cheerily, "wish me luck on a good sale. Goodbye Bill, we shall not meet again."

She went outside and loaded his bike into the rear of the Range Rover and then returned to lock the doors, humming the nursery rhyme that Selina had denied her.

She closed one half of the double doors and then began pushing shut the second.

The poison had seized Bill's throat and he rasped,

"Please leave the torch Caroline? Please, don't make me die in the dark."

"Don't be such a baby, Bill." Her face was framed in a strip of light.

"Please Caroline, please - I thought we were friends?"

Daylight narrowed from a wedge to a sliver and her final words were,

"My friend Bill? What an extraordinary notion that I should regard you as a friend."

The door clanged shut and plunged the tunnel into inky blackness.

He shouted one final time but the tunnel threw his voice back at him, jeeringly.

Bill heard the bolt scrape home, the padlock snap, and the sound of the engine as the Range Rover was driven away: it didn't sound lumpy at all.

# Chapter 18. Simon Brightwell Comes To Dinner

Simon Brightwell waited patiently in the cafe, playing with the crumbs of the custard tart and sipping the dregs of his coffee, unaware that Kevin Cory was watching to see if he had been followed either by an accomplice or a tail. Once satisfied that Brightwell was alone he telephoned him, inviting him to join him outside in his car. Brightwell sat beside the mystery vendor. He saw a big man, running away to fat around the middle but still strong and powerful, dressed casually in jeans and a sweater. He carried the confidence of being in charge. Kevin saw a city businessman - the sort of person he would describe as a townie.
"Long time" was all that Kevin said.
"Yes, let's go and talk" relied Simon.
"Our place for dinner."
They drove away from Yelverton shops to do the deal.

It was seven-fifteen pm, and night would soon be falling. Being the sort of Londoner who had no inclination for visiting the countryside, Simon was amazed that there were no street lights on the roads after leaving Yelverton, nor pavements. They had taken the Princetown road and then turned right onto a single track country lane. The tall grass hedges cut off any view of the surroundings and trees interlaced their branches overhead; they drove in what Simon thought of as a narrow green tunnel. It was going to be dark soon and everywhere would be pitch-black, silent, and very close to nature: too close for his liking. He liked lights and noise and cars, and a lot of people around him. Brightwell noted the isolation as Kevin Cory drove off the country lane and into a long private driveway marked Yennadon House, which was just stones and mud. They arrived at the house's own cattle grid, installed to prevent moorland stock from wandering onto the immaculate expanse of lawn. There were trees all around - tall and looming and still not fully in leaf - and the property was segregated from neighbouring houses: secluded behind its high hedges and shrubbery.

Brightwell had not expected to be whisked off to somewhere out of the way; he thought this vendor person would do business in an office - in a correct manner - with people passing by outside; he thought there would be red buses and taxis. They pulled up and stopped outside the front of Yennadon House and Brightwell appreciated both the value and refinement of the building. Then they walked through a porticoed doorway into a spacious hallway, and from there to a sitting room. It was a high ceilinged room with moulded cornices and walls decorated with expensive silk wallpaper with long matching drapes. High quality furniture finished the room, and a stone fireplace flared with a log-effect gas fire. Simon's first impression was, ' They may live in the country but they don't have mud on their boots. These people are accustomed to money and won't be easy to fool.'

'So this is the second envoy' thought Caroline as Kevin ushered Brightwell into their sitting room. She had dressed in a pink button-through long-sleeved dress, wanting to disarm with girly innocence. Brightwell was greeted by a professional lady who was attractive in a cool way.

His mind was in a spin. He wondered if these people had murdered Mister Leeden, remembering him in his lounge suit going off to catch the train to Plymouth. He knew he was a strong and fit man. How could this couple have pulled the wool over his eyes? Were they really capable of murder? If they admitted to having killed Leeden could he find it in himself to murder them? How would he do it? He was alone in a lonely location, in the home of two people suspected of murder, and only now did he realise the dire position in which he had placed himself. Then he reminded himself about the $3 million. He worked-out and was determined, and would use brute force and blunt instruments if needed - wrongly assessing Kevin as the deadliest - but he preferred to avoid violence and hoped to find that Leeden had come to, and gone safely from, this house. He really wanted to secure the agreement on the gold at the right price, get out unscathed, and go back to civilisation. Plymouth would do for the night but London was home. It was OK for Weismann to blithely talk about killing people but he, Simon, was looking at them in the flesh and wondering how to do it. He was a trader and longed to be away from all this mistrust and death: was not cut out for it.

Introductions were made and handshakes exchanged - all very professional.

"Please call us Caroline and Kevin will you Mister Brightwell? May we offer you an aperitif?"

Abi Cantrell had recently found out from the mortuary assistant that Mister Leeden had poison in his system so he would have to be extra careful on what he ate and drank.

"What are you having Caroline?"

"Gin and tonic."

"That will do me."

She went to a cocktail cabinet and Brightwell watched closely to see all three drinks poured from the same bottles.

"Shall we be seated?" said Caroline the urbane hostess. They made themselves comfortable. Brightwell noticed the aroma of dinner cooking and realised he had eaten nothing all day except a snack on the train down, and the custard tart at Yelverton. He was hungry.

"You have a lovely place here" he said, sticking to the banal for now.

Kevin sat in silence, wondering if this man had the clout to pull the deal together. The sums involved were colossal and he was intrigued about the mechanics of the exchange. His mind worked as a market trader – loading the van and setting the stall and how to present his sales pitch - he was sly and cunning but still operated at a rudimentary level. For all his wealth Kevin had never transitioned into being a real businessman, unlike others who had successfully followed his route to huge wealth; he remained a bottom-feeder with aspirations to be a Parish Councillor.

Kevin accepted his limitations and left the clever talk to his wife.
"What weather we have had Mister Brightwell, but spring is around the corner."
Caroline smiled and made more pleasantries but was ice-cold and under rigid control.

Between leaving Merriweather in the tunnel and cooking dinner she had decided to kill both Brightwell and Kevin and take the horde for herself. Kevin thought that being part of the first murder had made him part of the team, which meant he was too dangerous to let live; he'd become both smug and unreliable. While waiting for the men Caroline had used a syringe to inject paralysing agent into a potato which she would serve to Kevin – it was roasting separately in its own dish - but Brightwell would not have the poisoned dessert spoon until she witnessed Kevin eat this potato. She had crafted both drugs: Kevin's poison would kick in an hour later than Brightwell's because Kevin could do the donkey work and carry Brightwell's body into the Range Rover and then the tunnel; she had carried Kevin all these years hadn't she? Now it was payback. If the poison did not kill Kevin on cue she would let him have one of Mister Leeden's big fat bullets smack in the centre of his big fat back. Then his and Brightwell's bodies would be locked in the tunnel along with Merriweather and Jackson. Nice and neat.

It was six-thirty and more drinks were served, and some nibbles which Brightwell ignored in spite of his hunger. They sat around the fire chatting idly and watching each other as a hawk may watch a wary rabbit, quietly considering the when and how of murdering each other: she on when to kill both men - Brightwell on how to kill a husband and his wife - and Kevin along for the ride. Simon Brightwell cursed his stupidity in having not brought any form of weapon, and he eyed a heavy glass ashtray which he imagined would be enough to break Kevin's skull. Between pleasantries and small-talk he gauged the thickness of Caroline's slender pale neck, wondering how much force it would need to strangle her? At one stage he visualised Kevin lying inert with his blood pooling on the carpet while he choked the life from Caroline - her eyes and tongue bulging as she struggled beneath him - then the absurdity of it made him want to laugh hysterically, and he had to get a grip: what a pleasant evening.

Ж

It was seven in the same evening when Frank Steadwell received the oddest telephone call in her life from Selina's night-duty nurse, and she made the caller repeat herself.
"Did you say Selina Leigh *asked* for me? She actually *spoke*?"
"Yes, the third time Inspector, Selina has spoken and asked for that nice Steadwell police lady. You had better get here quickly though – she's going in and out of consciousness.".
Frank telephoned Robin and was then at Selina's bedside in ten minutes, extremely worried by her pallor and laboured breathing. Selina came-to and smiled, but something was restricting her breathing and she laboured to speak.

"I'm finished Mrs Steadwell and wanted to thank you for being so kindly."

"Telephone Professor Cory and get her here" she snapped to Robin.

"We don't have her number - she doesn't like being disturbed at home" the nurse interrupted.

"Then telephone Matron Miller – I assume she's not so picky?" Frank left the bedside and went searching for the professor's number – rattling her locked office door and peering through the venetian blind. Light from the corridor was shining through and she saw something that made her eyes widen. Selina's death certificate was lying on the desk together with an undertaker's business card. The nurse returned to say there was no reply from Matron.

"Let it ring for ten minutes. Now get the key to this office or I shall break the door."

Ж

The strip-light hung by a cable and Matron's mobile phone rang beneath a layer of dust and handfuls of banknotes. Storm Haven's basement was a chaos of scaffolding bars, timbers, and plaster; the air swirling with settling motes. Gruyere Cheese is fine until all the holes line up and then disaster follows. The cellar's roof had a huge gap through which the living room floor could be seen, but the cellar's occupants were seeing nothing. Stan and Marion Miller lay dead beneath tonnes of rubble. The strip-light fell and the tube shattered as her phone rang on in pitch blackness.

Ж

Rich meat and gravy wafted as beef was served onto plates at random and without preference. The three sat evenly spaced around the large table. Kevin kept his silence.
Brightwell opened, "I want my visit to benefit us all."
Caroline responded, "We thought you had lost interest when the first gentleman never got back to us. Do you still want to talk about a deal, Simon?"
As she spoke she offered both men vegetables.
"Oh Caroline, one never loses interest in the finest commodity on Earth. As for our mutual acquaintance, let us say he did not report everything back to us as fully as he should. I assume the quantity is still one tonne?"
"It is."
"How did you come into possession of the gold?"
"The gold will not cause you any problems, Mister Brightwell."
"Is this consignment encumbered by certification or other official interest?"
"Entirely not."
"Have you approached anyone else to sell it to?"
"No."
"I wish to purchase the consignment and I am able to offer you a mix of used banknotes in Stirling, Euros, and US Dollars, to the combined value of fifteen million dollars."

"Your first envoy must have relayed our disappointment in that figure when you know the true value is more than twice that. Did he not tell you?"

She spooned peas.

"My client believes this a fair price for taking the whole shipment."

"In the meanwhile I had considered finding another buyer, Mister Brightwell."

Brightwell did not scoff which made Caroline believe there were other buyers in the gold market. Kevin remained silent and started to eat. Caroline placed the poisoned potato close to the other vegetables, but slightly to one side.

"Do you know the whereabouts of our first friend?" enquired Brightwell.

"No, he said he would let us know but we heard no more from him."

Simon Brightwell took heart from this last piece of information - this was his ticket out of this madhouse once he had secured the gold. There followed a game of 'pass the vegetable dish' with Brightwell silently insisting they go first. When satisfied they had a bit of everything he took some and the meal began. Caroline was very subservient to her husband and helped him to food, which he ate with gusto – thus the poisoned potato was gulped down. They finished the main course and now for dessert and the poisoned spoon. The Cory's went first with dessert and then Brightwell, who scooped trifle and Devon clotted cream into his bowl; he ate and then licked his spoon clean. It was done – two killings for the price of one.

Dinner ended and the diners moved back to the sitting room for coffee and brandy, the talk continuing amiably while Caroline watched for breathing difficulty from her guest. They continue to haggled over the price and Kevin never spoke.
"I will have to see the complete tonne, you understand" said Brightwell.
"Of course" beamed Caroline, thinking 'and quicker than you imagine, Simon.'

※

An ambulance with flashing blue lights was speeding from the Drake Nursing Home carrying Selina to hospital. Robin accompanied Selina on this life-or-death run, carrying a bottle of clear liquid Frank had found in Caroline Cory's desk, which the A&E doctor wished to analyse. After the ambulance had gone Frank obtained the home address of Caroline Cory saying to herself, 'I want a word you, bitch.'

※

Bill Merriweather was close to death and hallucinating about two rescuers coming into the tunnel; they ignored him and left, relocking the door. Dying was bad, but worst still was Caroline calling him a baby…

*…Bill stared into the red-hot coals as his mother enquired how her dear little baby was. Only she could call him a baby*

*and he was happy to be with her again, sitting in his bath-tub in front of the kitchen land and staring into the coals. The coals were so red, but the centres were yellow and as he stared and stared they became gold. His mother asked, "Do you want to know about the gold, Bill?" What bliss. Bill was enveloped by the gold and his mind went right into the living centre of the hottest coal where there were no problems, just warmth and happiness…*

…and Bill Merriweather, janitor and handyman, gave the slightest of quivers and went over the edge. He died, happy.

Selina Leigh was close to death. Delirious, she hallucinated about the doctor in the white coat being her enemy…

*… Selina was a thirteen year old girl without a friend in the world – this man in white was coaxing her to talk, he was trying to get her to speak and tell about the gold. He may even be Dewer in disguise, sent by her father to take her down into Hell and burn her in the fires. The man in white injected her and she was hot all over - she was in the fires of Hell where the red-hot coals had yellow centres, so yellow they were golden, and she felt their awful heat…*

…Selina Leigh, institutionalised mute, gave the slightest of quivers and came back from the edge. She lived, unhappy.

# Chapter 19. Dénouement

Brightwell glanced from the flame-effect gas fire to the brandy, wondering which was making him feel so hot and dry. He said, "My client is well-respected and trustworthy. The money will be in used notes - you carry no risk and can start spending immediately - this alone is worth a considerable reduction."
"Mister Brightwell, I am not stupid and object to selling at half price."
Brightwell loosened his tie; his throat felt tight and he laboured for breath.
Caroline and a frowning Kevin exchanged the briefest glimpse. Brightwell continued his buyer's pitch, "Look, you have a tonne of gold to sell, and I want to buy it for my client. The price of gold fluctuates, and is dictated by circumstances..."
   They were interrupted by the ringing of the telephone. Caroline answered a man who spoke in English with a slight European accent,
"Put the telephone on loudspeaker, professor."
She disliked being instructed but this voice was wont to being obeyed and she did as she was told. Kowalski was a half-mile away speaking into a radio transmitter in the rear of the VW camper. His voice filled the room.
"I am Leonid Kowalski of Polish Military Intelligence but you will call me Colonel. I speak about the tonne of gold you so

casually discuss. It is not yours to sell or to buy – it belongs to Poland."

"Is this a joke?" Brightwell hissed, sitting up and scowling at Caroline.

"Do not interrupt or you will die the sooner. I am paying you the honesty of a dénouement before I dispose of this case, so that you fully understand why you have to be killed. Our gold was stolen from a house called Storm Haven at Yelverton, Mister Brightwell."

"At Yelverton?"

"Yes, we know the gold was once hidden there. The house was purchased by a family after the war and inherited by their daughter, a Mrs Paling. She knew the rumour of the gold but was principled and not interested. We know, because we have had a secret camera in Storm Haven's cellar for some years. I suspected the gold had been removed in 1945, but as Mrs Paling was not digging how could we know for sure? You could say she had innocently fenced the place off - paling - yes?" He waited for a laugh that never came.

"Mrs Paling died recently and a Stanislaw Miller purchased the house. This allowed us to fit a camera in the cellar and see how his diggings progressed. They have got nowhere. In fact the house just collapsed on him and his wife and has killed them both. It's a pity because Matron Miller, who was employed by Mister and Professor Cory, was desperate for money and I recruited her to spy on you, Caroline, for ten thousand pounds – she'd had half and would have received the balance in the next week, but never mind."

Kevin had a short attention span and went for a brandy.
"Be sure to regain your seat once you have the drink Kevin."
They looked for a camera but couldn't see one.
"It's well hidden - remember, we do this for a living - installed this afternoon when Kevin was meeting Brightwell and Caroline was following Merriweather to the gold's hiding place. After Caroline had left Bill to his fate we broke into the tunnel. It was marvellous to see our gold; wonderful. Merriweather was delirious but alive."
"Is he dead?" asked Caroline.
"Of course he's dead you foolish woman; he could not be allowed to live because he knew where our gold is. We fitted a camera and left him there - watched him die ten minutes ago - then switched it to infra-red and motion-activated. The battery will last until we move our gold to Poland. *Our gold* is firmly under *our* control."
"How did you know the gold had surfaced?" asked Caroline.
"A little spider in the centre of the international gold web reported a twang, at the same time as a man called Günter Weismann sent an assassin."
Brightwell stirred at Weismann's name but remained silent.
"I suppose him to be the body on Leeden Tor?" said Kowalski. "Because of this I had our camera in Storm Haven closely monitored. Stan Miller's burrowings and his conversations with Matron told me Selina was being pressurised by you, Caroline, into saying where the gold is - so I have been following you and today, like a nice little usherette, you took me straight to it."

Caroline was crimson with rage but Brightwell's curiosity had been replaced by a feeling of dread; Kowalski knew too much; he knew Weismann's identity which was very worrying indeed.

Kowalski asked, "Does Abigail Cantrell know about the gold, Mister Brightwell?"

"No, Colonel, if she knew she would have told me."

"Kevin, I understand that this Cantrell woman is your current peccadillo. Have you told her about the gold?"

"No Colonel, I have told no-one." This saved her life.

"What happens next, Colonel?" asked Caroline, tentatively.

"This afternoon, when we were in your empty house fitting our camera - which is crisply recording your last moments - we also clamped a bomb on the gas-storage tank in the cellar. It is a limpet mine of military-grade Semtex, containing titanium-coated steel balls that will rupture the tank and initiate a fireball of spectacular proportions. You are seated on your own funeral pyre."

Kowalski's finger hovered over a control box housing a single red button.

Brightwell began babbling, "I'm on an errand for Weismann and have nothing to do with the Polish gold - this was the first I knew of it - please sir, I will never mention it to anyone, please Colonel will you let me live?"

He dissolved into tears, and a snot bubble expanded from one of his nostrils.

"Mister Brightwell, you have been dealing in gold for many years but still do not understand it. It is the purest commodity know to humankind, but it corrupts those who covet it."

Kevin's cunning mind had turned to the windows and calculated the chances of flinging himself through but the double glazing made him abandon that idea - he thought of The Wizard of Oz and was Kowalski behind the curtains speaking into a funnel and pulling levers; it seemed a very funny idea - but then again?

Caroline was very cool but her brain was in overdrive: could she strike a deal with this Kowalski? "You must realise Colonel that I am of superior intellect and social standing to these two, and believe that you and I could work in partnership."

This way she could live and keep some gold for herself? Even a jumped up squaddie could see her worth, she thought.

The three, wrapped in their own thoughts, lived out their last few seconds.

Ж

It was a clear moon-lit night and Frank Steadwell stopped her car at the Cory's private drive. The gate was locked so she scrambled over and walked through darkness beneath trees. Burrator Reservoir was a sprinkle of reflected moonlight away to her left. She decided to take a short cut across the grass with the front lawn on her left and facing the right hand corner of the house. The outline of the house was visible with its ramp descending to the basement garage and a light shining through the hallway window. If Caroline was home the house gave no clue. Frank would knock the door, demand entry, and have the pleasure of arresting Professor Cory for the attempted murder of Selina Leigh.

She was halfway to the door when a shadow detach itself from the shrubs and a silhouette stealthily approach the house – the person was actually tiptoeing towards the front right-hand corner on a converging course to herself.

'Either a burglar or eves-dropper' thought Frank.

Suddenly a security light high up in one of the trees burst into stark brightness. The figure was almost at the main downstairs window when it abruptly turned and fled back in the direction it from which it had come. Frank saw Abi Cantrell, and Abi was in a funk. And then the house exploded. The ground shook beneath Frank's feet and glass scythed horizontally across the front lawn in glistening slivers. It disintegrated from inside out and a fireball like a miniature Hiroshima rolled into the sky and lighted the gardens like day. Frank was blown flat into some shrubs as the blast washed over her. The house had exhaled every last drop of air and it paused for breath, literally, drawing smoke and air back into the open-mouthed windows. Having caught its second wind the fire fed off cold, oxygen-rich air, which mixed with the contents of the pressurised gas-tank. A second and larger explosion turned the house into a rampant inferno. Distant car alarms were bleeping and wailing as debris began raining down. Frank rolled onto her side in time to see Cantrell frantically patting her head and hair, then collecting herself and running an unsteady exit. Had either woman been in the direct path of the blast they would have been shredded, but the angle of approach had saved both. Somewhere a dog was barking frantically: trees rustled with falling debris and burning embers spiralled to earth. A slate whizzed past Frank's ear to bury itself harmlessly into the lawn - it seemed an age but eventually the deadly rain stopped.

The sitting room had been invaded by a maelstrom of fire and building materials that had blown up from the basement and clean through the roof. Twisted out of shape the empty gas tank created a huge gap. More explosions followed from the vehicles' fuel tanks, burning tyres, paint cans, stored rifle ammunition, and the effects of mains-pressure water spraying over bare electrical cables. The cellar had become a huge fire-pit. The three occupants, pulverised by timbers and floorboards and furniture, were incinerated in the all-consuming fireball. Blackened and reduced beyond recognition they fell into the blazing cellar where the fire was most intense - fell into a gold centred hell-on-earth that reduced them to a conglomerate of ashes. Caroline Cory mixed her remains with that of her despised husband and a total stranger, and in a dirty hole in the ground she became a dirty pile of nothing.

# Chapter 20. Nice, Neat, and Cosy

"Poland is an old ally who stood with us during the dark days of the war Inspector Steadwell", the Assistant Chief Constable said sternly. Only twelve hours had passed since the fire and Frank had slept little, but she tried to look alert.
"This conversation is well off-the-record Inspector but the importance of the Cory's - a couple who ran a dubious residential home in which they had attempted the murder of an elderly patient - cannot be compared to that of the Republic of Poland."
Frank had supervised the removal of the three unrecognisable bodies labelled as Kevin and Caroline Cory and William Merriweather, and was wondering what she had done wrong.
"There can be no conflict in loyalty to our old friends and the thoroughness, *or otherwise Inspector*, of the investigation into the fire at the Cory residence. You should not be too analytical in your investigation. Accept what you see and follow the nuances of the enquiry without seeking further guidance from senior management."
Frank suspected Kowalski's hand had been involved in the explosion, and now it was obvious that the Polish Embassy had pulled strings at Whitehall.
She said nothing. End of a cosy interview.

Ж

Later the same day Frank was called to Her Majesty's Coroner to discuss the fire. She was astonished by what he said.
"I accept the identity of the three deceased without the requirement of formal identification, DNA analysis, or post-mortem examinations. Also, there will be no need to seek the opinions of a fire officer or gas engineer. I am opening the inquest into the deaths of Kevin Cory, Caroline Cory, and William Merriweather. I am satisfied Mr and Mrs Cory had befriended William Merriweather, an employee who looked after the boiler at their nursing home but who lacked certification and the training to do so. His pedal cycle and tool-kit were found in the remains of Yennadon House. It is apparent that he worked on the gas-tank and accidentally instigated a defect which caused an explosion and catastrophic fire. Merriweather was having dinner with his employers when the tank exploded and all three perished in a fatal accident brought about by lack of experience. I record accidental deaths and close this inquest." He peered over his spectacles.
"I'll be frank. We've both been around the maypole and led a merry dance to nowhere" she replied, completely satisfied that Kowalski's had murdered three people, but knowing her hands were tied.
"Yes, but I don't want to be pole-dancing for the rest of my career and neither do you. Good afternoon Inspector."
He returned to something more demanding on his desk and the matter was irrefutably closed. End of another cosy interview.

Ж

Nursing singed hair and hurt pride Abi squeezed past a temporary security fence to gain access Storm Haven's cellar. The steps down were filled with dust and plaster, and in the cellar there was a huge hole where the ceiling had been; she could see the fireplace in the room above and the edge of a carpet. The cellar was a chaotic mess and the remains of the ceiling hung precariously. She turned over debris, finding twenty pound notes, rifle bullets, and a crushed thermos-flask. There was dried blood in the dust where the Millers had lain. Then she felt a slight sensation and wondered if that was dandruff on her shoulder? Spills of dust were followed by a warning creak. Abi's exit was anything but dignified and she just cleared the steps as the ceiling fell in a white blizzard. Trembling, she sat in her car, 'This business has almost got me shot, then blown up, and now crushed. Brightwell refuses to answer calls and I still don't know what this is all about."

    She drove to Tavistock intent on answers and intercepted Robin over lunch in a café in Russell Street.
"Robin, who was Mister Leeden?"
"A dead body that sent us on a wild goose chase. Forget him Abi, really do."
"You left my cottage at daybreak just recently, and pretty fast; plenty of men fancy getting me to bed, and you had done, so what's wrong?"
"Abi, I'm gay."

"Why didn't you say so earlier? I wouldn't have wasted so much time. If you need male services I can find someone for a fee." And she meant it.

Plumping and preening she glided out on high heels and left him in peace.

"A nice, neat ending to what would have been a very demanding affair" thought Robin, who was hugely relieved.

Then Abi received a telephone call from the London police about a missing person called Simon Brightwell. Her number had figured in some of his telephone calls.

"We met in an online chat-room" she lied.

Truthfully she said she'd never physically met him, although she'd unknowingly been within kissing distance outside the cafe at Yelverton.

The police told her that going walkabout is not an offence, and they were closing Brightwell's file as 'missing and whereabouts unknown.'

Abi thought Brightwell had gone to ground and fretted about the thousands of pounds that she could miss out on. Kowalski intercepted her calls and accepted she knew nothing about the gold: lucky her.

Ж

"Suzi dear it's me. Want an update?"
"All ears Abi darling."

"I've had the cops onto me about Brightwell. Seems he's gone missing but I managed to fob them off. Pity about the money, but there you are."

"What about your DS boyfriend?"

"Robin is a bit more than a boyfriend now, having spent a night of bliss with me. He's just tried dumping me on the pretext of being gay, but I saw straight through that of course. The way he looked me up and down was enough to confirm that he's hooked."

"Got his phone number?"

"Better than that dear, I've got his phone which he left at my place the other night. When I tell him I have it he'll have to pay me another visit, won't he?"

"What else?"

"Not much in sleepy Tavistock dear; been shot at, almost blown up, and just escaped a house falling on my head. Apart from that it's all pretty slow."

Suzi thought she was joking, and asked, "Are you busy at work?"

"There has been a fire and explosion and the owners of the Drake Residential Home have been killed, and I have been appointed the interim manager by the solicitor who is winding up their estate. The owner was Professor Caroline Cory and guess what? She has been careless and misplaced her passport and driving licence - the applications for replacements were posted by me yesterday, both bearing my photograph. Well a girl must always have a Plan B, mustn't she?"

⚜

High in the tree-tops they twisted to watch the solemn procession - then the jackdaws cawed and flapped off. Gravel crunched as the undertaker walked ahead of three coffins. No black tails or top hats, no flowers or cards, no mourners for Caroline or Kevin and the misidentified Bill Merriweather. They were buried under windswept trees at Walkhampton Church and not far from the unmourned Harold Leigh. Later, Stan and Marion Miller would join them in the ground - five earth mounds socialising in death. That same day the remains of the Cory household was bulldozed into the cellar and grassed over; all nice and neat just as Caroline had liked.

⚜

Those steely eyes glittered as he poured wine, his strong square hands confident in whatever he did. 'Handsome but arrogant' though Frank, and not for the first time where Kowalski was concerned. They were having lunch again – his invitation – at the Bedford Hotel. A glass wall flooded the room with light and crisp white linen adorned the tables.
Frank waited for the reason for the invitation, which was not long in coming.
"Something my country owns has come back to my possession. I shall move it when convenient. It would be better if you forgot this matter."
"Are you threatening a Police Officer?"

"If I had reason to threaten, you would not be alive. I give friendly advice."
"Your advice suits the world that you live in. You live a life completely different to other people - so at odds with any normal society - that you have lost sight of humanity. I never wanted your precious gold to start with; I wanted to get to the bottom of who a dead man was. You may find this difficult to accept in a system driven by objectives and goals, but that dead man belongs to someone; they all belong to someone. My appetite has deserted me. Goodbye Colonel."
She left, paying her half of the bill on the way out. Frank was getting particular from whom she accepted hospitality. She was also growing tired of cosy little interviews.

Ж

Frank and Robin were having the final case review.
"How did you shake off Abi?"
"I told her I'm gay."
"Are you?"
"No, but I couldn't scorn her, could I?" Although playing stupid Robin kept quiet about his night with Abi. He couldn't chase her from his mind. It had been a heavenly experience and she was fabulous - but a walking disaster. He hoped she didn't try tempting him back though, because he might dissolve completely.

Ж

Frank had found a self-contained flat for Selina - one with a daily help. She could afford it because the money her father had in the old tin pot had grown to a huge sum. Selina now had a credit card and new clothes, had joined ladies groups and was taking reading lessons; her power of speech had developed hugely. Selina had her own life but the thing she really wanted was to be baptised, and she got her way.
The clean, cold water had the effect of washing Leigh Farm from Selina's soul and she was hugely uplifted. After the ceremony Selina and Frank walked to the new graves; she lingered at the one containing Brightwell, believing the occupant to be Merriweather, and she was sad – Bill had never harmed her and she had always had a soft spot for him. Kevin's grave she ignored, as he'd ignored her.

Selina moved on and stopped at Caroline's grave; she stood with a quizzical smile.
"If she had her way I would be down there and her up here. Caroline wanted me to say a nursery rhyme at a meeting of her hospital people to show how clever she was. But clever people can be so stupid, Frank. I'll recite it…"

> *Humpty Dumpty sat on a wall,*
> *Humpty Dumpty had a great fall,*
> *All the King's horses and all the King's men,*
> *Couldn't put Humpty together again.*

                                                                    ...and
                        how thick is that?"

Selina went next to her mother's grave where Frank left her alone, and finally she came to that of her father. From the carrier she brought out a glass flower vase which she propped beside his headstone, then a pressurised gas lighter and a box of large cigars. She spread cigars into a bouquet in the vase – then played flame over their tips, lighting them. Thirteen cigars, one for each of the years she was with him, and for each of the scars he had burned into her body.
"I'm baptised so Dewer can't take me to Hell. Have this final smoke on me Stinkface and I hope it chokes you."

The two women walked back and at the cars embraced like sisters. Frank handed Selina a plastic bag and she drove off. Selina gave instructions to the taxi driver – she still had two more things to do.

# Chapter 21. Weismann

Lake Geneva twinkled in the distance as Weismann stared through the window of the exclusive Japanese restaurant, where he was dining alone. He wondered for the hundredth time about Brightwell's silence. Where was he and did he have the gold? The tightly bound sushi made him think of fat rolls of money. Sushi suited Weismann who could select fastidiously and without commitment, and he was fussily occupied when a waiter approached with a telephone. Speaking French the waiter said, "Someone for Mr Weismann who will not identify himself but says it is very important."

Frowning at the interruption Weismann snatched the handset and spoke in French but was answered by a man speaking German with a Polish accent – Weismann was conversing with Kowalski, who was in the rear of the orange VW parked at a service area on the English M5 motorway.

"Mr Weismann, my name is Leonid Kowalski and I am a Colonel in Polish Military Intelligence. I speak to you about a quantity of gold in which you are interested – a tonne of gold – yes?"

"Continue."

"You have entered into business with a man from Ankara who has the highest ambitions in leadership –aspirations not matched by his principles."

"I am a businessman, and the business of business is business."

"I'm surprised that a Jew can be involved with someone who peddles humankind under vile conditions. The Turk brings people to the West as slaves and prostitutes or unwilling organ donors; furthermore, he brings them in cattle trucks where they suffer as the Jews suffered in cattle trucks - as your grandfather would have suffered had he not escaped from the Nazis. Are you not ashamed?"
"Do you want money?"
"Money will not buy me. I want you to drop The Turk and never speak with him again. Also, forget all about Storm Gold; it is not yours – understood?"
Weismann looked around a dining room full of rich, well-dressed people. Fine wines and crystal stood on spotless table-linen and waiters obsequiously attended them with *haute cuisine*. No-one was taking notice in him, nor using a phone.
"Where are you, Kowalski?"
"In England where I have recovered the gold; now listen and do not interrupt. Never contact The Turk again and forget about the gold or you will lose your life. Remember this well - goodbye." He rang off.
Weismann was outraged to be threatened here in neutral Switzerland – it was preposterous – a Pole in England could not touch him here. He knew some very unpleasant people and Kowalski would be sorry. Telling the waiter he would return he went out to the restaurant car-park and entered his expensive car. The door hushed shut like the closing of an airlock onto an inviolable space. It was quiet and plush and Weismann settled into the cream calf-leather and opened the

central consul, bringing out the substantial in-car telephone. Its screen illuminated his face.

One hundred metres away a black car was parked in such a way that Weismann was observed by the two occupants - one female and the other male. They were Kowalski's people. The woman watched Weismann through a monocular and the man held a small black box with a glowing red button. Their satnav had been adapted and as Weismann pushed the keypad on his telephone the same number appeared on their satnav: it was the telephone number of The Turk. Weismann placed the carphone to his right ear - it rang - was picked up and a voice answered; the red button was pushed on the black box and three ounces of Semtex detonated inside Weismann's earpiece. The watchers witnessed a brief flash and a slight percussion as Weismann's car alarm blared. Six steel balls the size of peppercorns transferred at sonic speed from earpiece to ear to Weismann's brain, killing him instantly. The woman rang Kowalski. "As you predicted Colonel, he ran straight into the arms of his friend from the other side of The Bosporus. He is no more I assure you." The call ended and Kowalski said to the field agents in the VW, "He couldn't be allowed to live but his final act reinforced my suspicions about The Turk. We are finished for the present here in England and I will see you back in Poland."

Alone in his car Kowalski studied a photograph of the tattoo **Ъ7Ж3Ø**. The marks were from the Cyrillic alphabet meaning Mister Leeden could have been a field agent in special squad from Russia or Eastern European. His best guess was on a highly-trained operator who had retired - or turned renegade and been expelled - and then gone freelance. A mercenary lone wolf is always the most difficult to pin down. Kowalski suspected the tattoo was esoteric and exclusive to members of an arcane cell making it intentionally meaningless to outsiders. Both he and Steadwell had wasted time on the tattoo; time and effort. It was what the English call a red-herring and furthermore it had worked. Mister Leeden - the man and his body - had become a complete red-herring and obfuscation had heaped enigma onto mystery. Leeden would remain persistently obscure and beyond reach; a perplexing closed-book. They shouldn't have been investigating him at all but the man who'd sent him and why: but the gold had been recovered and he, Kowalski, had pulled off a good job. Not that Kowalski was his real name – even his wife didn't know his real name.

# Chapter 22. Dewerstone

Selina told the taxi driver to wait on a country parking spot, near a place called Cadover Bridge. She began walking a deserted track across rough grass on common land, with the carrier bag in hand. On her left was a deep wooded valley, already in shade, and beneath the canopy of trees flowed the River Plym. Away to her right the sun was lowering in the western sky. Shadows cut across her path and she continued to a hilltop with far views. Selina had often wondered what the Dewerstone was like – the ambush place of Dewer himself – and after so many years she was here. A fresh breeze blew through stunted trees and the quiet was unbroken. Dewerstone had been an ancient hill-fort with a huge drop on one side. She stood beside craggy peaks that rose from more than a hundred feet below, their tips bathed pink by the sun. A densely wooded valley on the other side of the River Plym was their backdrop. She realised this was the first time since childhood that she had been really alone and then remembered why she had come.

Selina reached tentatively into the bag as though wary of being bitten or grabbed. Her fingers felt the dry crackle of old paper, weather stained and crisp. Pulling out the hateful drawing of Dewer and the Wisch Hound she held it up to the dying sun. His eyeholes blazed with sunlight and the dog followed its master's cue. How damp her bedroom smelled, how the wind howled and the tin roof bumped - she was instantly back there - feeling the rough floorboards beneath her bare feet, sensing the lonely moor outside her window and hearing *him* shouting for a light for his smoke. Numbness gripped her stomach - how sinister those sun-blooded eyes were, those four sinister pools that had watching her unblinkingly in her own little bed. She snapped out of her sick dream, frightened and alone. There could be no escape, even now. Skin crawling and clammy she shook with terror and her resolve evaporated. Then a voice inside her head – it could have been her dead mother talking to her down the years – said, "If you want freedom Selina, you must do it." Selina coached herself, her mind shook free the spell and her head came up. He'd pushed lighted cigars through those eyeholes and burned her flesh - had mocked her helplessness.

Turning away from the sun Selina held up the drawing to the light, looking at Dewer and his hound illuminated stark red as though looking from Hell's flames - Dewer with leering mouth and clawed hand and the hound ready to do his bidding. "You can't have me now – I'm baptised – so go to Hell on your own."

The lighter flared with a clean blue flame. She lifted it to Dewer, seeing for the first time he was only crayon on dry paper: that he was nothing. She burned out Dewer's eyes - saw them enlarge in shock as she took charge - then burned out his whole face before turning her attention to the hound. The paper crisped and when well alight she let the breeze take it high above Dewerstone. It disintegrated into a shower of sparks. He was not Dewer after all, only paper – she'd been terrified by a

piece of paper. Reaching back in the bag she was surprised how the remaining item fitted into the palm of her hand, ugly yet familiar considering she had never touched it in her life. Pulling out his billhook she turned it this way and that. The metal was scratched and discoloured and it was an evil sullen lump just as her father had been evil and sullen; she hated his billhook as she'd hated him. The setting sun was a blood-red disc as Selina drew back her arm and flung the billhook with all her might, all her venom and pent-up anger, up and over the Dewerstone. It paused at the apex of her throw – stained red by the dying rays - and hung menacingly like a bloody claw, before lazily tipping over the arc to fall silently to the cleansing river below. Free at last, she spat the words, "Goodbye Dewer – Goodbye Stinkface."
Darkness was falling and somewhere a solitary dog gave a long and mournful howl.

Ж

At the same moment that Selina threw her past over The Dewerstone, Frank Steadwell was a few miles away on the top of Leeden Tor and casting her mind over the lives this gold had claimed. Frank counted off Kevin and Caroline Cory, Stan and Marion Miller and, for the wrong reason, Bill Merriweather. Kowalski alone knew the full picture and could have added John Jackson, the obscure Mister Leeden, Simon Brightwell, and now Günter Weismann: at this stage even Kowalski didn't know The Turk would be added to the list. In three months he would have to eliminate the Turk – have him murdered - because the Turk's obsession with the gold would prove so irksome he could no longer be ignored. Had the Turk stuck to crime and let politicians run politics he would have lived a lot longer, but not even Kowalski could have foreseen this turn of events. From Kowalski the future of men was hidden. Only the Nether-Gnome of Crazywell Pool knew such things.

Ж

Selina had one more thing to do and gave the taxi driver the address of Police Constable Len Dennis; retired.

## 23. King's Man

Selina sat opposite Len Dennis in the conservatory.
"You haven't that changed much Len."
"You have Selina – you were only thirteen."
"I spent all those years in homes watching people talk, listening to TV and radio, wanting to talk but stopping myself. I played the thirteen year old with Professor Cory to keep her cruelty at bay. Len, why are there evil people in the world?"
"Evil people exist to show us how not to be."
"Bill Merriweather was kind and gave me a kitten. I always liked Bill - had a soft spot in my heart for him - and he for me."
"Well girl, blood is thicker than water, as you know - no you don't know, do you? John Jackson was no good for his wife and Jenny Jackson had a void in her centre that was filled by Harold Leigh – he got her pregnant and Bill Merriweather was the outcome, but she called the child Merriweather after some dead pilot she never knew, thinking he would stand a better chance in life than being a Jackson. No one would admit to being an offspring of Harold Leigh now would they? Oh, sorry Selina, but you know what I mean. Anyhow, you had a soft spot for Bill because he was your half-brother."

This was a stunning revelation but it was not the reason for Selina's visit and she took the bull by the horns.
"Do you remember when I came into your police station that day in 1947?"

"How could I forget? It's not often a little girl in a thin dress and scuffed shoes walks into a police station to say she's killed her father by deliberately pushing a wall on him."

"I remember sitting on your motor cycle, holding onto you with one hand and trying to keep the wind out of my skirt with the other. Bumping along the farm track and taking you back to see his body. I felt so free with the breeze in my hair and him gone."

"We both had a shock when we got to the farm, Selina."

"The biggest shock ever…"

*…Constable Dennis parked his motorbike beside the fallen wall and they got off. The wall was six feet high and where the collapse had occurred it looked like a breached dam had emptied across her father's back, or perhaps a giant had taken a huge bite and spat the stones over him. His legs were covered by granite, and also his left arm. A great heap of the rocks rested on his back and the only visible parts were his head and right arm. Blood had pooled below his mouth and his right arm was crooked up beside his face and was broken - it was at a funny angle and there were bluish bumps beneath the skin - and in his hand he gripped the billhook. She could clearly see where she'd burned him with the cigar when he was unconscious; could see the round black hole in his inner forearm. The cigar was on the ground two or three feet from away where she'd thrown it.*

*Taking the Constable's hand in both hers she gently pulled him towards the body. They knelt beside her father's putty-coloured face, looking into his open, staring eyes. The constable and Selina went closer and closer until they were looking right into them – and then Harold Leigh's eyes flickered and focussed. They jumped out of their skins when he came back. At first she thought it could be a nervous reaction but then he snarled, "Get these stones off me Selina Leigh." At first Stinkface ordered, but when that didn't work he began to wheedle and use mock kindness, telling her what a good girl she was and how he appreciated her. She knelt with her hands clasped over her mouth, frozen with a bewilderment that was swiftly followed by the fear. Could he, would he, get out from under the stones – have her there all to himself to shout at and torture with his cigars? Then Harold Leigh made the biggest mistake of his entire life, "Your poor mother would have been so proud of you Selina"...*

...talking about my mother was the final straw and something snapped. I went to the field and searched for a big stone. It was difficult to pick it up but I struggled with it and walked along his torso. It was like carrying the next part of a pier that was under construction except I didn't drop the stone into the sea, I let it smash down onto that huge broad back. There was a crack followed by a scream. I'd never heard him scream – didn't know he had it in him – and I hopped down to look. Blood was bubbling and frothing from his mouth and he was trying to grip the billhook, but the broken arm had sapped all his strength; even then he clung to his billhook like a big baby to its dummy. Now he was helpless - like the defenceless little child I had been so many times."

She paused, then, "Do you remember where you were, Len?

"I went and sat astride my motorbike because it was a familiar object in the chaos. I sat and did nothing - worse - I allowed you to wreak vengeance on him."

"He was massive and powerful and the stone hadn't killed him so I went for another. My dress was covered in mud and I'd lost a shoe but nothing could stop me then. Staggering back I dropped it on him, and this time he begged for mercy – mercy from *me*, his little whipping girl – Stinkface wanting a bit of pity from *his* Selina. Not a chance. There was a puddle of blood in the earth and his speech was slurred but he was still fighting for life. It took a third stone to finish the job. I went and got the biggest I could lift – one that was part buried by the mud and it sucked as I tugged it free. Shuffling across his back I spoke to him one last time – do you remember what I said Len?"

"You said, 'Here's one for you Dewer - come and get him' and you dropped that stone onto the back of his head with a blood-chilling thud. He gave a massive groan, twitched and dropped the billhook."

"I'd done it - he really was dead that time" answered Selina.

"You were drained and blaming yourself – not only for killing him but for not having the courage to leave before it came to this. Crying and rocking beside his body and saying you should have walked out years before and stopped his awfulness by not being there – that it was all your fault. But I was the one to blame. I was a policeman and had taken an oath to King George the Sixth - I was the King's Man - and should have pursued his crime spree, should have chased him down relentlessly, but hadn't. That's why I never stopped you killing him; you'd done what I couldn't and I stood back and let you. I had taken my oath of duty to be a King's Man, in which I was derelict."

"Len, you were one of the King's Men and Stinkface was Humpty Dumpty."

"Selina, he'd had a great fall alright, and you made sure and all the king's horses and all the kings men, couldn't put Humpty together again."

"And there we were with him between us, dead."

"You were in a terrible state so I had to think for you - had to take charge - and that meant controlling the crime scene and you, the witness. First, the stones on him were piled up like a pyramid so I pulled them off like they'd rolled away naturally. It had to seem that the stones had fallen in a single collapse, not a series of drops, had to look right for the CID. Then I picked up his cigar and dropped it into the crook between his forearm and mouth – how could he have been burned on the arm by a cigar that had been flung several feet aside?"

"You were very particular, Len."

"Stepping back I ran a critical eye over him; it all looked OK - it had to - it was 1947, murder was a capital offence and as an accessory I could be tried as a principle offender. You would have escaped the executioner but they would have hanged me for sure - would have taken me for a nine o' clock walk one morning and dropped me. So, we had to have our story right." Len's mind was back at the scene.

"You had to say, Selina, that the wall fell without warning with you nowhere near it; that you had tried to get the stones off and that's how your dress got all muddy. The cigar had burned his arm and you brushed it free. They'd know from his post mortem he'd been conscious after being pinned, so you'd have to say you struggled with the stones but were too weak - make it sound convincing."

"It was like a dream with me in my dirty dress and one shoe, him dead and staring with the billhook beside his hand, and you a policeman in uniform schooling me in how to tell lies and beat the law. I was nothing to you Len and you had your duty to do. So why did you lie for me?"

"Two reasons – First, you'd done the world a favour getting rid of him. Second, when you were sitting there so miserable and lost I saw the burns he'd put on your arms and legs - raised ugly scars, plum-red with dry and flaky edges. That's when I decided to help you. I hated him for his arrogance and the way he destroyed other peoples' lives. I hated Harold Leigh for all the pain he'd caused – a hatred that was deep in the pit of my stomach. I was pleased to see him face down in the mud and his power undone – pleased he was dead and gone."

"But I couldn't get my lines right Len, and you told me to say nothing and be silent – to stay mute and no-one could prove anything. Stinkface always told me to stay silent and you'd done the same. The two most important men in my life had told me to say nothing. So it was settled and I did that for all of my life – I said nothing. I thought killing him would free me from his prison but it locked me in another."

"It imprisoned us both Selina – you in a series of institutions and me inside my conscience. We were thrown together in a crazy situation; it was other-worldly and I still have difficulty believing it happened. One moment I was a county copper doing his bit and the next the ground had moved under my feet. I made my choice that day and lived with it but I've carried the stain. It's been my burden all my life. Meeting you has made it all different - our confessions have purged our souls and I'll tell no-one what happened all those years ago. Now I can face death with a clear conscience and intend taking our secret to the grave. But what about you Selina? You still have a life to live."

She knelt beside him and hugged him close, whispering, "Thank you Len for risking everything - your career, your good name, your very life – all to help a helpless girl who'd landed on your doorstep. You were not a bad man - you were a hero who helped carry my burden." They held each other tight as tears spilled down their faces. Then Selina broke away with a sardonic smile playing on her lips.
"But on the subject of my father's death - and if it's all the same to you constable - I will continue for the rest of my life to be Mute of Malice."

The End.

Printed in Great Britain
by Amazon